/英・檢・保・證・班/

全民英檢 初級 保證班

閱讀與寫作 題庫

三大特色
- 完全配合英檢試題
- 模擬試題實戰演練
- 掌握英語學習要領

英檢過關 Easy Go！

初碧華 /著

書泉出版社 印行

序

▼ 你常因英文不好而沮喪嗎？

▼ 你常想要學好英文，可是卻不知如何「下手」嗎？

▼ 你常被文法搞得焦頭爛額、心煩氣躁嗎？

▼ 你常寫不出一句簡單實用的英文嗎？

▼ 你常想用英文敘述簡單的事件卻困難重重嗎？

▼ 你常想放棄英文，可是學校、公司卻不願放你一馬嗎？

▼ 還是——你自覺英文不錯，但卻不知如何準備英檢考試呢？

如果你有以上困擾的話，那麼這本書鐵定會讓你眼睛為之一亮，重新燃起對英文的信心。

如果站著看這本書有點累，那就買回家看吧！因為在家裡，不管是躺著看，坐著看，趴著看，蹲著看，還是倒立著看，你都會發現這是一本不可多得的好書，因為這本書具有四大特色：

1. 文法解說清晰，切中要點—— Terrific！
2. 題型掌握確實，切中核心—— Fantastic！
3. 解題技巧獨到，切中要害—— Fabulous！
4. 題目練習逼真，切中紅心—— Marvelous！

熟讀本書，英文必然突飛猛進，考試更能輕鬆過關。

初碧華

目錄
Contents

第一組

Part I

Practice Test 1

第一章 試題卷

1 閱讀能力測驗

本測驗分三部分，全為四選一之選擇題，共 35 題，作答時間 40 分鐘。

第一部分：詞彙和結構

本部分共 15 題，每題含一個空格。請就試題冊上 A、B、C、D 四個選項中選出最適合題意的字或詞，標示在答案紙上。

Questions 1～15

1. We have known each other since we ＿＿＿＿ ten.
   A. are
   B. were
   C. have been
   D. be

2. France is ＿＿＿＿ for its food and wine.
   A. comfortable
   B. careful
   C. famous
   D. convenient

3. Mark is ＿＿＿＿ student in his class.
   A. taller
   B. tallest
   C. the taller
   D. the tallest

4. Lucy is _____ in jogging and swimming.
   A. interest
   B. interesting
   C. interested
   D. interests

5. Would you turn on the light? I'm afraid _____ the dark.
   A. of
   B. for
   C. at
   D. with

6. It _____ me a week to finish this report.
   A. takes
   B. took
   C. spends
   D. spent

7. I'll call you as soon as I _____ there.
   A. get
   B. got
   C. will get
   D. will get to

8. Jenny _____ in a car accident the other day.
   A. hurt
   B. hurts
   C. was hurt
   D. was hurted

9. The woman _____ by the window is my aunt.
   A. who stands
   B. who's standing
   C. stands
   D. stood

10. Please don't _____ the same mistake again.
    A. do
    B. get
    C. take
    D. make

11. Mary looked _____ at her little brother.
    A. angry
    B. angrily
    C. happy
    D. unhappy

12. The baseball game was _____ because of the rain.
    A. put on
    B. put off
    C. put down
    D. put up

13. My mom is a good cook. She always cooks _____ food.
    A. funny
    B. dangerous
    C. delicious
    D. exciting

14. You must try the stinky tofu before you _____ tomorrow.
    A. will leave
    B. leave
    C. left
    D. to leave

15. _____ you don't hurry up, we will miss the school bus.
    A. If
    B. When
    C. Before
    D. Although

第二部分　段落填空

本部分共 10 題，包括二個段落，每個段落各含 5 個空格。請就試題冊上 A、B、C、D 四個選項中選出最適合題意的字或詞，標示在答案紙上。

Questions 16～20

Linda Jackson was 25 years old. She was from Chicago but lived in New York. One day, she met Michael Wilson, 28, an engineer, at a pub. They liked each other at first sight. The next day, Michael asked Linda （16）. They had a wonderful dinner at Top Gun, the best restaurant in town. （17）, when Michael wanted to pay the bill, he found that he had lost his wallet. So, Linda paid it （18）. After dinner, they went to a movie, （19） Linda didn't enjoy very much. Then Michael took Linda to the beach. As soon as they （20） there, it began to rain. They had to hurry back to the car. It was not a smooth date for both of them.

16. A. out
    B. in
    C. off
    D. on

17. A. Because
    B. Although
    C. Therefore
    D. However

18. A. instead
    B. wonderfully
    C. carefully
    D. though

19. A. what
    B. who
    C. which
    D. where

20. A. arrived in
    B. arrived at
    C. got to
    D. got

Questions 21~25

Frank is ⟨21⟩ a soccer team and teaches soccer at high school. In his free time, he likes to play Scrabble, a game of words. It's well-known in many countries. You can get Scrabble in 23 languages. Each person in the game has seven letters. Players use their letters ⟨22⟩ words and get points. For example, you get one point for the letters L, I, or E and five points for the letter K. So the word "like" is ⟨23⟩ eight points.

"It's easy to learn Scrabble. People can have fun and ⟨24⟩ their English at the same time," says Frank. At home, Frank teaches his son to play Scrabble. Sometimes he invites his friends or neighbors over for the game of Scrabble. Their games often ⟨25⟩ several hours.

21. A. on
    B. in
    C. at
    D. for

22. A. spell
    B. spelled
    C. spelling
    D. to spell

23. A. worth
    B. worthy
    C. getting
    D. needing

24. A. prepare for
    B. work on
    C. study for
    D. depend on

25. A. spend
    B. spent
    C. take
    D. took

第三部分　閱讀理解

本部分共 10 題，包括數段短文，每段短文後有 1～3 個相關問題，請就試題冊上 A、B、C、D 四個選項中選出最適合者，標示在答案紙上。

Question 26

• **Please Keep Off the Grass** •

26. Where would you most probably see this sign?
   A. In a hotel.
   B. In a hospital.
   C. In a park.
   D. In a mall.

Questions 27～28

To: Nina
From: Derek
Date: Mar. 21
　　Could you wake me up at 7:30 a.m. tomorrow? My alarm clock is broken, and I have to see a doctor at 9:00. Thanks a lot.

27. **What time does Derek need to get up?**
    A. 7:30 tomorrow morning.
    B. 8:00 tomorrow morning.
    C. 7:30 tomorrow evening.
    D. 8:00 tomorrow evening.

28. **Why does Derek ask Nina to wake him up?**
    A. Because he always sleeps late.
    B. Because Nina is a hotel clerk.
    C. Because his alarm clock is not working.
    D. Because he wants Nina to prepare breakfast.

Questions 29~30

Single, Male, 27

I'm looking for my ideal woman. I'm 175cm and 65kg. In my free time, I love playing basketball, singing, listening to music, and going to the movies.

If you're a single woman, aged 20-25, who enjoys being with a humorous man, then you're the one.

Please e-mail to peterchen@ms20.hinet.net

29. Where would you most likely see this advertisement?
    A. At a supermarket.
    B. In a hospital.
    C. At a bus stop.
    D. In a newspaper.

30. Which is not true?
    A. The man is looking for a woman aged 20-25.
    B. Singing is one of the man's hobbies.
    C. The man is not fun to be with.
    D. The man has an e-mail address.

Questions 31~32

One day in Chicago, six million dollars fell out of a truck that turned over around a corner. Suddenly there was money everywhere on the street. Some people filled their bags with money, some people put the money in their pockets, and some people even took off their coats to hold the falling money. Everybody was busy picking up the unexpected money.

A few hours later, the police officers went from door to door to ask for the lost money, but no one returned. The people there believed that God sent the money to them. However, two weeks later, a mail carrier returned one hundred thousand dollars to the police.

31. So far how much money has been returned?
    A. $6,000,000.
    B. $1,000,000.
    C. $10,000.
    D. $100,000.

32. Why did the police officers go from door to door?
    A. To find the owner of the lost money.
    B. To catch the thieves.
    C. To ask people to return the money.
    D. To tell people to stay indoors.

Questions 33~35

Dear Andy,

I haven't heard from you since March. What happened? Is your computer out of order, so you can't reach me? Did you get my picture? How do you like me in the picture? My sister, Lucy, said I looked great.

As I mentioned last time, you look just as I thought. After spending hundreds of hours chatting with you, I have become so close to you. I'm sure you feel the same way. We know all about each other such as our likes and dislikes. Do you know how excited I was when you said you were crazy about me last time? To tell the truth, I'm still excited about that now.

Well, I'm going to Taipei next Saturday. Can we meet then? I'm looking forward to seeing you soon. Do write to me soon.

Missing you,

Amy

33. Who is going to Taipei next week?
    A. Andy.
    B. Amy.
    C. Lucy.
    D. Not sure.

34. How do Andy and Amy keep in touch?
    A. By phone.
    B. By mail.
    C. Through the Internet.
    D. Not sure.

35. Which of these is not true?
    A. Amy is fond of Andy.
    B. Andy hasn't written Amy for quite a while.
    C. Andy and Lucy are brother and sister.
    D. Andy once told Amy that he was crazy about her.

2 寫作能力測驗

第一部分　單句寫作

請將答案寫在寫作能力測驗答案紙對應的題號旁，如有拼字、標點、大小寫之錯誤，將予扣分。

第 1～5 題：句子改寫

> 請依題目之提示，將原句改寫成指定型式，並將改寫的句子完整地寫在答案卷上（包括提示之文字及標點符號）。

1. Miss Lin taught her students nicely.
   Did _____?

2. John goes to the movies once a week.
   How _____?

3. Where is Jenny?
   Please tell me _____.

4. To pass the test takes a lot of work.
   It _____.

5. This pen is more expensive than that one.
   That pen _____.

第 6～10 題：句子合併

請依照題目指示，將兩句合併成一句，並將合併的句子完整地
寫在答案卷上（包括提示之文字及標點符號）。

6. Do you hear it?
   John is singing in the bathroom.
   Do _____?

7. Do you know the woman?
   The woman is talking on the phone.
   Do _____?

8. Mike hurt his foot.
   He was playing basketball.（用 while）
   _____.

9. Lisa lives in Taipei.
   Eva lives in Taipei, too.（用 both）
   _____.

10. Mark started to play computer games at 9:00.
    He is still playing them.（用 since）
    _____.

第 **11～15** 題：重組

> 請將題目中所有提示字詞整合成一有意義的句子，並將重組的
> 句子完整地寫在答案卷上（包括提示之文字及標點符號）。答
> 案中必須使用所有提示字詞，且不能隨意增加字詞，否則不予
> 計分。

11. **They** _____.
    yesterday / hurry / left / in / a

12. **Landy** _____.
    has / piano / been / the / ten / playing / years / for

13. **An active reader** _____.
    on / a time / usually / one thing / concentrates / at

14. **She** _____.
    teacher / most / English / the / popular / at / school / is

15. **What** _____!
    smart / he / a / is / boy

第二部分　段落寫作

請依照題目要求，寫一篇約 50 字的段落。本部分採整體式評分
（0～5 級分），再轉換成百分制。評分要點包括重點表達的完整
性、文法、用字、拼字、字母大小寫、標點符號。

題目：
**昨天你在路上看到一起交通事故，請根據圖片寫一篇約 50
字的短文，來描述你所看到事件的經過。**

第二章　解析卷

1 閱讀能力測驗

本測驗分三部分，全為四選一之選擇題，共 35 題，作答時間 40 分鐘。

第一部分　詞彙和結構

本部分共 15 題，每題含一個空格。請就試題冊上 A、B、C、D 四個選項中選出最適合題意的字或詞，標示在答案紙上。

Questions 1～15

1. We have known each other since we _____ ten.
   A. are
   B. were
   C. have been
   D. be

   答案：（B）

   中譯：我們從十歲就認識到現在。

   解析：此題考 since 的用法，其句型如下：
   S + have/has + p.p. + since + S + V過去式
   S + have/has + p.p. + since + 特定過去時間
   由... since we _____ ten. 得知空格須填「動詞過去式」，
   而複數形 be 動詞（are）的過去式為 were。
   其他例句參考如下：
   ① I have lived in Taipei since I was six.
      我從六歲開始就住在台北。
   ② Two years have passed since he left.
      他離開已經有兩年了。
   ③ He has worked here since 2000.
      他從西元二千年就在這裡工作了。

since 的其他句型參考如下：

S + have/has + been + V-ing + since + S + V過去式
（表示到目前還在持續進行中）

S + have/has + been + V-ing + since + 特定時間
（表示到目前還在持續進行中）

① Joe has been watching TV since 2:00 in the afternoon.
　Joe 從下午兩點就一直看電視看到現在。

② Betty has been playing the piano since she came home.
　Betty 從回家以後就一直彈鋼琴彈到現在。

此外，since 尚有下列兩種用法：

It + is/has been + 一段時間 + since + S + V過去式

S + have/has + p.p. + since + 一段時間 + ago

① It is/has been three years since Mary left Taiwan.
　Mary 離開台灣已有兩年之久。

② She has eaten nothing since two days ago.
　她已經兩天沒吃東西了。

2. **France is ＿＿＿＿ for its food and wine.**
   A. comfortable
   B. careful
   C. famous
   D. convenient

答案：（C）

中譯：法國以美酒佳餚聞名。

解析：此題考「用字」：
　　　A. comfortable　舒適的；自在的
　　　B. careful　小心的
　　　C. famous　著名的
　　　D. convenient　方便的
　　　根據上述，只有 C. 符合語意，所以答案應選 C. famous（著名的）。
　　　※ **be famous for**：以…聞名。

3. Mark is _____ student in his class.
   A. taller
   B. tallest
   C. the taller
   D. the tallest

答案：（D）

中譯：Mark 是他班上最高的學生。

解析：由 ... in his class 可知此題考 「最高級形容詞」的用法，
　　　所以答案只能選 D. the tallest。

4. Lucy is _____ in jogging and swimming.
   A. interest
   B. interesting
   C. interested
   D. interests

答案：（C）

中譯：Lucy 喜歡慢跑和游泳。

解析：此題考 interest 的用法，其句型如下：
　　　人 + be interested in + 事物
　　　事物 + be interesting to + 人
　　　事物 + interest + 人
　　　I'm interested in swimming.
　　　= Swimming is interesting to me.
　　　= Swimming interests me.
　　　我對游泳感到興趣。我喜歡游泳。

5. Would you turn on the light? I'm afraid _____ the dark.
   A. of
   B. for
   C. at
   D. with

答案：（A）

中譯：能否請你把燈打開？我怕黑。

解析：此題考單字 **afraid** 的用法：

be afraid of + N/V-ing 害怕…

be afraid that + S + V 恐怕…

① I'm afraid of dogs.

我怕狗。

② I'm afraid that I can't go to your party.

我恐怕沒辦法參加你的派對。

6. It _____ me a week to finish this report.

A. takes

B. took

C. spends

D. spent

答案：（B）

中譯：我花了一個禮拜的時間才完成這個報告。

解析：此題考 **take/took** 和 **spend/spent** 的用法，其區別如下：

It + took + 人 + 時間 + to + V

人 + spent + 時間 + V-ing

① It **took** me twenty minutes to walk home.

我花了二十分鐘走路回家。

② John **spent** all day playing computer games.

約翰花了一整天的時間在玩電腦遊戲。

③ It **will take** me two weeks to organize a meeting.

= I will spend two weeks organizing a meeting.

籌組會議將花掉我兩週的時間。

7. I'll call you as soon as I _____ there.

A. get

B. got

C. will get

D. will get to

答案：（A）

中譯：我一到那裡就打電話給你。

解析：此題考 as soon as（一…就…）引導「副詞子句」的用法：

S + will + V + as soon as + S + V（現在式）

S + V過去式 + as soon as + S + V過去式

由題目 **I'll call** you as soon as I _____ there. 得知空格應填「動詞」現在式以代替未來式，所以答案應選 A. get。

8. Jenny _____ in a car accident the other day.

A. hurt

B. hurts

C. was hurt

D. was hurted

答案：（C）

中譯：Jenny 前幾天車禍受傷。

解析：此題考 **hurt** 的用法：

① Don't hurt the dog.

別傷害那隻狗。

② My foot hurts.

我的腳會痛。

③ He was hurt.

他受傷了。

由題意得知空格須填「被動式」，所以答案應選C. was hurt（受傷）。

9. The woman _____ by the window is my aunt.

A. who stands

B. who's standing

C. stands

D. stood

答案：（B）

中譯：站在窗戶旁的那位女士是我的姨媽。

解析：此題考「關係子句」（形容詞子句）的用法。其中主要子句為 **The woman is my aunt.** 形容詞子句為 _____ by the window. 由於先行詞是「人」，所以關係代名詞須為 **who**。以消去法砍去 C. stands 及 D. stood，剩下 A. who stands 及 B. who's standing。由於談論的對象是屬於「目前所見」的情況，所以其動作須用「現在進行式」，推而得知答案應選 B. who's standing。另外，題目亦可簡化為「分詞」用法，亦即 The woman **standing** by the window is my aunt.

10. **Please don't _____ the same mistake again.**

    A. do

    B. get

    C. take

    D. make

    答案：（D）

    中譯：請不要再犯同樣的錯誤。

    解析：此題考「搭配詞」的用法：**make** a mistake（犯錯）。

11. **Mary looked _____ at her little brother.**

    A. angry

    B. angrily

    C. happy

    D. unhappy

    答案：（B）

    中譯：Mary 生氣地注視她的小弟。

    解析：此題考「副詞」的用法：

    look at + O + Adv = look + Adv + at + O

Don't look at me angrily.

= Don't look angrily at me.

不要怒視我。

【比較】

You look beautiful **in** that dress.

= That dress looks beautiful **on** you.

你穿那件洋裝很好看。

12. The baseball game was _____ because of the rain.

A. put on

B. put off

C. put down

D. put up

答案：（B）

中譯：棒球賽因雨延期。

解析：此題考「片語」用法：

　　　A. put on　穿上

　　　B. put off　延期

　　　C. put down　放下；寫下（＝write down）

　　　D. put up　舉起；掛起；建造

　　　依題意，答案應選 B. put off（延期）。另外，put up with

　　　= stand（忍受）。

13. My mom is a good cook. She always cooks _____ food.

A. funny

B. dangerous

C. delicious

D. exciting

答案：（C）

中譯：我媽媽是個好廚師，她總是做美味的食物。

解析：此題考「單字」用法：
　　　A. funny　好笑的；奇怪的
　　　B. dangerous　危險的
　　　C. delicious　美味可口的，好吃的
　　　D. exciting　刺激的，過癮的，令人興奮的
　　　依據題意，答案應選 C. delicious（美味的）。

14. You must try the stinky tofu before you _____ tomorrow.
    A. will leave
    B. leave
    C. left
    D. to leave

答案：（B）

中譯：你明天離開前，務必去嚐一下臭豆腐。

解析：此題考「現在式」代替未來式的副詞子句用法：
　　　① I'll call you as soon as I **get** there.
　　　　我一到那裡，就打電話給你。
　　　② Let's get together before you **leave** tomorrow.
　　　　你明天離開前，讓我們聚一聚。
　　　③ We will probably be eating dinner when you **come** tomorrow.
　　　　你明天來的時候，我們可能正在吃飯。
　　　依據上述例句的文法規則，答案應選 B. leave。

15. _____ you don't hurry up, we will miss the school bus.
    A. If
    B. When
    C. Before
    D. Although

答案：（A）

中譯：如果你不快一點，我們就會錯過校車。

解析：此題考「從屬連接詞」的用法：

　　　A. If　如果

　　　B. When　當

　　　C. Before　在…之前

　　　D. Although　雖然

　　　根據題意，答案應選 A. If（如果）。

第二部分　段落填空

本部分共 10 題，包括二個段落，每個段落各含 5 個空格。請就試題冊上 A、B、C、D 四個選項中選出最適合題意的字或詞，標示在答案紙上。

Questions 16~20

> Linda Jackson was 25 years old. She was from Chicago but lived in New York. One day, she met Michael Wilson, 28, an engineer, at a pub. They liked each other at first sight. The next day, Michael asked Linda （16）. They had a wonderful dinner at Top Gun, the best restaurant in town. （17）, when Michael wanted to pay the bill, he found that he had lost his wallet. So, Linda paid it （18）. After dinner, they went to a movie, （19） Linda didn't enjoy very much. Then Michael took Linda to the beach. As soon as they （20） there, it began to rain. They had to hurry back to the car. It was not a smooth date for both of them.

16. A. out
    B. in
    C. off
    D. on

17. A. Because
    B. Although
    C. Therefore
    D. However

18. A. instead
    B. wonderfully
    C. carefully
    D. though

19. A. what
    B. who
    C. which
    D. where

20. A. arrived in
   B. arrived at
   C. got to
   D. got

答案：16.（A）　17.（D）　18.（A）　19.（C）　20.（D）

中譯：

> 　　Linda Jackson 當時二十五歲。她來自芝加哥，但住在紐約。有一天，她在酒館遇見 Michael Wilson，二十八歲，是一名工程師。他們彼此一見鍾情。隔天，Michael 約 Linda 外出。他們在當地最好的一家餐館 Top Gun（捍衛戰士餐廳）享受一頓美好的晚餐。然而，當 Michael 要付帳的時候，他發現皮夾不見了。因此，就改由 Linda 付帳。吃完晚餐後，他們去看電影，不過 Linda 不太喜歡那部電影。接著，Michael 帶 Linda 去海邊。他們一到那裡，便開始下雨，他們只好匆匆回到車上。對他們兩個來說，這次約會真是不順利啊！

解析：

16. ask sb. out　約某人外出，等於 ask sb. out on a date。

17. 此題考「副詞」用法，由上下文得知空格須填一表示「反意」或「驚訝」的字，所以只能選 D. However（然而）。

18. 此題考用字：
   A. instead　代替（為 Adv，可放句首或句尾）
   B. wonderfully　奇妙地
   C. carefully　小心地
   D. though　雖然；但是，儘管如此（放句尾，且前有逗點）
   根據上述，只有 A. instead（代替）符合語意。

19. 此題考關係代名詞，由於先行詞為 **movie**，屬於事物，所以答案只能選 C. which。而 B. who 的先行詞須為人，D. where 的先行詞須為地方。A. what 屬關係代名詞之變形，如 This is what we want.（這是我們所要的），He is not what he was.（他已不是從前的他了），於此亦不合。

20. 此題考「動詞」到達 與「副詞」there 之用法。
    A. arrived in　後接大地方，如 Taipei
    B. arrived at　後接小地方，如 the station
    C. got to　後接大小地方，即等於 arrived in/at
    所以答案只能選 D. got。
    另外，選項 A. B. C. 只要把介系詞 in, at, to 去掉，即可成為正確答案。亦即 **arrived there, got there** 即可。

Questions 21～25

　　Frank is ＿(21)＿ a soccer team and teaches soccer at high school. In his free time, he likes to play Scrabble, a game of words. It's well-known in many countries. You can get Scrabble in 23 languages. Each person in the game has seven letters. Players use their letters ＿(22)＿ words and get points. For example, you get one point for the letters L, I, or E and five points for the letter K. So the word "like" is ＿(23)＿ eight points.

　　"It's easy to learn Scrabble. People can have fun and ＿(24)＿ their English at the same time," says Frank. At home, Frank teaches his son to play Scrabble. Sometimes he invites his friends or neighbors over for the game of Scrabble. Their games often ＿(25)＿ several hours.

21. A. on
    B. in
    C. at
    D. for

22. A. spell
    B. spelled
    C. spelling
    D. to spell

23. A. worth
    B. worthy
    C. getting
    D. needing

24. A. prepare for
    B. work on
    C. study for
    D. depend on

25. A. spend
    B. spent
    C. take
    D. took

答案：21.（A）　22.（D）　23.（A）　24.（B）　25.（C）

中譯：

　　Frank 是足球隊員，同時也在高中教足球。空閒的時候，他喜歡玩拼字遊戲。這遊戲在很多國家廣為人知。它有二十三種語言版本。參賽者有七個字母，他們用這些字母拼字得分。例如，字母 L、I 或 E 代表一分，而 K 代表五分，所以拼出單字「like」就得八分。

　　「拼字遊戲很容易學。人們可以邊玩邊練習英文。」Frank 說道。在家裡，Frank 教他兒子玩拼字遊戲。有時候，他還邀朋友或鄰居到家裡來玩拼字遊戲。一玩就常常要耗上幾個鐘頭。

解析：

21. 參加球隊介詞須用 on。

22. S + use + O + to + V　使用…來做…

23. 此題考「用字」：
    S + be + worth + N 或 Ving　…值（得）…
    B. worthy 後須有 of + N（值得），C. getting 及 D. needing 用進
    行式很怪，且語意不合。所以答案只能選 A. worth。

24. 此題考「片語」用法：
    A. prepare for　準備
    B. work on　練習；解決；研究
    C. study for　準備，為…而唸書
    D. depend on　依賴
    由上下文得知只有 B. 符合語意。

25. 此題考「用字」：
    事物 + take +（某人）+ 時間　事物花某人多少時間
    人 + spend + 時間 + V-ing/on + N　某人花多少時間從事…／
    　　　　　　　　　　　　　　　　　在…之上

    所以答案只能選 C. take。

第三部分 閱讀理解

本部分共 10 題，包括數段短文，每段短文後有 1～3 個相關問題，請就試題冊上 A、B、C、D 四個選項中選出最適合者，標示在答案紙上。

Question 26

> • **Please Keep Off the Grass** •

26. Where would you most probably see this sign?
   A. In a hotel.
   B. In a hospital.
   C. In a park.
   D. In a mall.

第 26 題

> • **請 勿 踐 踏 草 皮** •

26. 題目：此告示牌最可能出現的地點為何？
   選項：A. 旅館。
      B. 醫院。
      C. 公園。
      D. 購物中心。
   答案：（C）

Questions 27~28

> To: Nina
> From: Derek
> Date: Mar. 21
> Could you wake me up at 7:30 a.m. tomorrow? My alarm clock is broken, and I have to see a doctor at 9:00. Thanks a lot.

27. What time does Derek need to get up?
    A. 7:30 tomorrow morning.
    B. 8:00 tomorrow morning.
    C. 7:30 tomorrow evening.
    D. 8:00 tomorrow evening.

28. Why does Derek ask Nina to wake him up?
    A. Because he always sleeps late.
    B. Because Nina is a hotel clerk.
    C. Because his alarm clock is not working.
    D. Because he wants Nina to prepare breakfast.

第 27～28 題

給：Nina
留言者：Derek
日期：三月二十一日
　　明天早上七點半叫我起床好嗎？我的鬧鐘壞了，而我九點要去看醫生，多謝。

27. 題目： Derek 幾點必須起床？
　　選項： A. 明早七點半。
　　　　　 B. 明早八點。
　　　　　 C. 明晚七點半。
　　　　　 D. 明晚八點。
　　答案：（A）

28. 題目： Derek 為什麼要 Nina 叫他起床？
　　選項： A. 因為他總是睡得很晚（晚起）。
　　　　　 B. 因為 Nina 是旅館職員。
　　　　　 C. 因為他的鬧鐘壞了。
　　　　　 D. 因為他要 Nina 做早餐。
　　答案：（C）

Questions 29~30

Single, Male, 27

I'm looking for my ideal woman. I'm 175cm and 65kg. In my free time, I love playing basketball, singing, listening to music, and going to the movies.

If you're a single woman, aged 20-25, who enjoys being with a humorous man, then you're the one.

Please e-mail to peterchen@ms20.hinet.net

29. Where would you most likely see this advertisement?
    A. At a supermarket.
    B. In a hospital.
    C. At a bus stop.
    D. In a newspaper.

30. Which is not true?
    A. The man is looking for a woman aged 20-25.
    B. Singing is one of the man's hobbies.
    C. The man is not fun to be with.
    D. The man has an e-mail address.

第 **29～30** 題

> # 單身，男性， 27歲
>
> 　我正在尋覓理想伴侶。我身高一百七十五公分，體重六十五公斤。平常有空的時候，我喜歡打籃球、唱歌、聽音樂和看電影。
>
> 　如果你是單身女性，年齡介於二十到二十五歲之間，喜歡和幽默男性相處的話，那妳就是我的真命天女。
>
> *請 e-mail 到 peterchen@ms20.hinet.net*

29. 題目：你最可能在哪裡見到這則廣告？
    選項：A. 在超市。
    　　　B. 在醫院。
    　　　C. 在公車站。
    　　　D. 在報紙上。
    答案：（D）

30. 題目：下列何者為非？
    選項：A. 這名男子正在尋覓年齡介於二十到二十五之間的女性。
    　　　B. 唱歌是該名男子的嗜好之一。
    　　　C. 這名男子並不風趣。
    　　　D. 這名男子有電子信箱。
    答案：（C）

Questions 31～32

One day in Chicago, six million dollars fell out of a truck that turned over around a corner. Suddenly there was money everywhere on the street. Some people filled their bags with money, some people put the money in their pockets, and some people even took off their coats to hold the falling money. Everybody was busy picking up the unexpected money.

A few hours later, the police officers went from door to door to ask for the lost money, but no one returned. The people there believed that God sent the money to them. However, two weeks later, a mail carrier returned one hundred thousand dollars to the police.

31. So far how much money has been returned?
    A. $6,000,000.
    B. $1,000,000.
    C. $10,000.
    D. $100,000.

32. Why did the police officers go from door to door?
    A. To find the owner of the lost money.
    B. To catch the thieves.
    C. To ask people to return the money.
    D. To tell people to stay indoors.

第 31～32 題

> 　　某一天在芝加哥市，一部卡車於街道轉角處翻覆，結果有六百萬美金掉了出來。突然間，路上到處都是鈔票。有些人拿袋子裝錢，有些人把錢塞進口袋，甚至還有人脫下大衣來裝掉落的錢。大家都忙著撿這些意外之財。
>
> 　　幾個小時之後，警員們挨家挨戶去要回這些遺失的鈔票，但是沒有人歸還。當地人認為這些錢是上帝送給他們的禮物。然而，兩星期後，有一名郵差歸還了十萬元鈔票給警方。

31. 題目：到目前為止，有多少錢被送回來？
　　選項：A. 六百萬元。
　　　　　B. 一百萬元。
　　　　　C. 一萬元。
　　　　　D. 十萬元。
　　答案：（D）

32. 題目：為何警方要挨家挨戶去探訪？
　　選項：A. 為了尋找鈔票的失主。
　　　　　B. 為了逮捕小偷。
　　　　　C. 為了要求人們歸還鈔票。
　　　　　D. 為了告知人們不要外出。
　　答案：（C）

Questions 33~35

Dear Andy,

I haven't heard from you since March. What happened? Is your computer out of order, so you can't reach me? Did you get my picture? How do you like me in the picture? My sister, Lucy, said I looked great.

As I mentioned last time, you look just as I thought. After spending hundreds of hours chatting with you, I have become so close to you. I'm sure you feel the same way. We know all about each other such as our likes and dislikes. Do you know how excited I was when you said you were crazy about me last time? To tell the truth, I'm still excited about that now.

Well, I'm going to Taipei next Saturday. Can we meet then? I'm looking forward to seeing you soon. Do write to me soon.

Missing you,
Amy

33. Who is going to Taipei next week?
    A. Andy.
    B. Amy.
    C. Lucy.
    D. Not sure.

34. How do Andy and Amy keep in touch?
    A. By phone.
    B. By mail.
    C. Through the Internet.
    D. Not sure.

35. Which of these is not true?

A. Amy is fond of Andy.

B. Andy hasn't written Amy for quite a while.

C. Andy and Lucy are brother and sister.

D. Andy once told Amy that he was crazy about her.

第 33～35 題

親愛的 Andy,

　　自從三月以來，我就沒有你的消息。到底怎麼了？難道是你的電腦故障，所以無法跟我連絡？你有收到我的照片嗎？覺得我還上相嗎？我姊姊（妹妹）Lucy 說我很上相。

　　我上次有說過，你看起來跟我想的一樣。跟你聊天聊了幾百個小時之後，感覺跟你好親近喔！我相信你也有同樣的感覺。我們彼此了解，像是我們的好惡，也都十分清楚。你知道嗎？當你上次跟我說你對我痴狂的時候，我是多麼地興奮啊！老實說，到現在我還是很興奮。

　　嗯，下週六我要去台北，到時能否碰個面？期待能很快見到你。務必儘快寫信給我。

想你的

Amy

33. 題目：誰下週要去台北？

　　選項：A. Andy。

　　　　　B. Amy。

　　　　　C. Lucy。

　　　　　D. 不確定。

　　答案：（B）

34. 題目：Andy 和 Amy 如何保持聯繫？
    選項：A. 透過電話。
    　　　B. 藉由通信。
    　　　C. 透過網路。
    　　　D. 不確定。
    答案：(C)
    解析：由第一段 Is your computer out of order, so you can't reach me? 得知。

35. 題目：下列何者為非？
    選項：A. Amy 喜歡 Andy。
    　　　B. Andy 很久沒有寫信給 Amy。
    　　　C. Andy 和 Lucy 是兄妹／姊弟。
    　　　D. Andy 曾經告訴 Amy 他很喜歡她。
    答案：(C)
    解析：Amy 和 Lucy 是姊妹。

2 寫作能力測驗

第一部分　單句寫作

請將答案寫在寫作能力測驗答案紙對應的題號旁，如有拼字、標點、大小寫之錯誤，將予扣分。

第 1～5 題：句子改寫

> 請依題目之提示，將原句改寫成指定型式，並將改寫的句子完整地寫在答案卷上（包括提示之文字及標點符號）。

1. Miss Lin taught her students nicely.
   Did _____?
   答案：Did Miss Lin teach her students nicely?
   中譯：林老師很有耐心地教她的學生嗎？
   解析：此題考含助動詞的 **Yes-No** 疑問句之用法，其句型如下：
   Do/Does + S + V原形?（現在式）
   Did + S + V原形?（過去式）
   ① Do you have time tomorrow?
      你明天有空嗎？
   ② Does she need help?
      她需要幫忙嗎？
   ③ Did you study for the math test yesterday?
      你昨天有準備數學考試嗎？
   ④ Did John call you last night?
      John 昨晚有打電話給你嗎？
   ※ 過去式不管第幾人稱，助動詞一律用 **Did**。
      疑問句的相關句型及例句，請參考姊妹作《全民英檢初級保證班》「文法要點4」疑問句。

2. John goes to the movies once a week.

How _____?

答案：How **often does John go to the movies**?

中譯：John 多久去看一次電影？

解析：由句尾 **once a week**（一週一次）得知此題考某事發生之頻率，其句型如下：

How often do/does + S + V?

① A: How often does Tom play basketball?

   B: He plays basketball twice a week.

   A：Tom多久打一次籃球？

   B：他一個禮拜打兩次籃球。

② A: How often do you go bowling?

   B: Once a month.

   A：你多久打一次保齡球？

   B：一個月一次。

3. Where is Jenny?

Please tell me _____.

答案：Please tell me **where Jenny is**.

中譯：請告訴我 Jenny 人在哪裡。

解析：此題考名詞子句的用法，其句型如下：

S + V (+ O) + wh-word + S + V

① I don't know where she is.

   = Where is she? I don't know.

   我不知道她人在哪裡。

② Please tell me what you want.

   = What do you want? Please tell me.

   請告訴我你要什麼。

※ 相關例句及用法請參考姊妹作《全民英檢初級保證班》「文法要點 **12**」子句或「寫作題型全都錄」。

4. To pass the test takes a lot of work.

It _____.

答案：It takes a lot of work to pass the test.

中譯：要通過考試需要相當的努力。

解析：此題考慮主詞與不定詞的用法，其句型如下：

It is + Adj/N + to + V

= To + V + is + Adj/N

It takes + N + to + V

= To + V + takes + N

① It is exciting to watch basketball games.

　= To watch basketball games is exciting.

　看籃球賽很過癮。

② It takes time to learn English well.

　= To learn English well takes time.

　學好英文需要花時間。

③ It is my pleasure to work with you.

　= To work with you is my pleasure.

　跟你共事是我的榮幸。

以上例句亦可改成動名詞形式：

① **Watching** basketball game is exciting.

② **Learning** English well takes time.

③ **Working** with you is my pleasure.

5. This pen is more expensive than that one.

That pen _____.

答案：That pen **is cheaper than this one.**

　　= That pen is less expensive than this one.

　　= That pen is not so/as expensive as this one.

中譯：那支筆比這支便宜。

解析：此題考形容詞比較級的用法，其句型如下：

S1 + be + more + Adj（三音節或以上）**+ than + S2**

S1 + be + less + Adj（三音節或以上）**+ than + S2**
S1 + be + Adj-er（二音節或以下）**+ than + S2**

① Lisa is more beautiful than Jenny.

= Jenny is less beautiful than Lisa.

Lisa 比 Jenny 好看。Jenny 比 Lisa 醜。

② Johnny is taller than Henry.

= Henry is shorter than Johnny.

Johnny 比 Henry 高。Henry 比 Johnny 矮。

第 6～10 題：句子合併

請依照題目指示，將兩句合併成一句，並將合併的句子完整地寫在答案卷上（包括提示之文字及標點符號）。

6. Do you hear it?

John is singing in the bathroom.

Do _____?

答案：Do you hear John singing in the bathroom?

中譯：你有聽到 John 在浴室裡唱歌嗎？

解析：此題考感官動詞（如 see, hear）後接動詞的用法，其句型如下：

S + see/hear + O + V-ing（強調動作的進行狀態）

S + see/hear + O + V（強調動作的發生與結束）

① I saw Mike **enter** a bank yesterday.

昨天我看見 Mike 進入一家銀行。

② I hear them **singing** in the next room.

我聽見他們在隔壁房間唱歌。

7. Do you know the woman?

The woman is talking on the phone.

Do _____?

答案：Do you know the woman (who is) talking on the phone?

中譯：你認識在講電話的那個女人嗎？

解析：此題考形容詞子句的用法，其關係代名詞選用規則如下：

who：先行詞為人。

which：先行詞為事物。

where：先行詞為地方（= in which）。

when：先行詞為時間。

whose：先行詞為所有格。

whom：先行詞為受格。

that：先行詞為人、事物（= who, which）。

由於句子的先行詞為「人」（the woman），所以關係代名詞須用 who。合併句子為：Do you know the woman who is talking on the phone? 亦可簡化成：Do you know the woman talking on the phone?

8. Mike hurt his foot.

He was playing basketball.（用 while）

_____.

答案：Mike hurt his foot while he was playing basketball.

= While Mike was playing basketball, he hurt his foot.

中譯：Mike 打籃球時弄傷了腳。

解析：此題考 while（當）的用法，時態屬過去進行式，其句型如下：

While + S + was/were + V-ing, S + V過去式

= S + V過去式 + while + S + was/were + V-ing

While I was jogging in the park, I lost my wallet.

= I lost my wallet while I was jogging in the park.

當我在公園跑步時，我遺失了皮夾。

過去進行式的其他句型參考如下：

When + S + V過去式, S + was/were + V-ing

① When Michelle arrived, we were having dinner.

= We were having dinner when Michelle arrived.

Michelle 到的時候，我們正在用晚餐。

② When Nina called last night, I was taking a shower.

= I was taking a shower when Nina called last night.

Nina 昨晚打電話來的時候，我正在洗澡。

9. Lisa lives in Taipei.

Eva lives in Taipei, too.（用 both）

_____.

答案：Both Lisa and Eva live in Taipei.

中譯：Lisa 和 Eva 兩個都住在台北。

解析：此題考 **both** 的用法，其句型如下：

Both + A + and + B + V

Both + A + and + B + be...

① Both John and Mary study hard.

John 和 Mary 兩個都很用功。

② Both Ben and Wendy are smart.

= Ben and Wendy are both smart.

Ben 和 Wendy 兩個都很聰明。

③ Both of them are married.

= They both are married.

= They are both married.

他們兩個都已結婚。

④ Both of them are not married.

他們兩個並非都已結婚。（即一個結婚，一個未婚。）

※ **Neither of them is married.**

他們兩個都還沒結婚。

10. Mark started to play computer games at 9:00. He is still playing them.（用 since）

_____.

答案：Mark has been playing computer games since 9:00.

中譯：Mark 從九點就開始玩電腦遊戲。（到現在還在玩。）

解析：此題考 **since** 的用法，其句型如下：

S + have/has + been + V-ing + since + 過去時間

（強調還在進行當中）

S + have/has + p.p. + since + 過去時間

（強調到目前為止所完成的動作）

① My younger brother has been playing computer games since 2:30.

我弟弟從兩點半就開始玩電腦遊戲。（到現在還在玩）

② I haven't heard from Brenda since January.

我從一月到現在都沒有Brenda的消息。

※ **since** 的其他用法請參考姊妹作《全民英檢初級保證班》「文法要點3」時態。

第 11～15 題：重組

> 請將題目中所有提示字詞整合成一有意義的句子，並將重組的句子完整地寫在答案卷上（包括提示之文字及標點符號）。答案中必須使用所有提示字詞，且不能隨意增加字詞，否則不予計分。

11. They _____.

yesterday / hurry / left / in / a

答案：They **left in a hurry yesterday.**

中譯：他們昨天匆匆離開。

解析：重組題目一般先從五大基本句型及四大變化句型著手，
接著再以時態對應即可。

本題主詞為 They，動詞為 left，修飾語 in a hurry（匆
忙），時間副詞 yesterday 可放在句首或句尾，但一般放在
句尾居多。所以答案為：They left in a hurry yesterday.
屬五大基本句型中的第一型：**S + V**。

※ 其他句型及用法請參考姊妹作《全民英檢初級保證班》
「文法要點 1」一招半式闖江湖及「段落寫作 2」段落文
章必殺句型。

12. Landy _____.

has / piano / been / the / ten / playing / years / for

答案：Landy **has been playing the piano for ten years**.

中譯：Landy 彈鋼琴已有十年之久。

解析：從關鍵字 has, been, playing 得知此題考現在完成式的用
法，其句型為：

S + have/has + been + V-ing + for + 一段時間

S + have/has + been + V-ing + since + 過去時間

① I have been playing video games for six hours.
我打電動已經打了六個小時。（目前還在打）

② She has been playing the piano since 9:30 in the
morning.
她從早上九點半就在彈鋼琴。（現在還在彈）

13. An active reader _____.

on / a time / usually / one thing / concentrates / at

答案：An active reader **usually concentrates on one thing at
a time**.

中譯：一個積極的讀者通常一次只專注做一件事。（即不會分心）

解析：先抓片語 concentrate on（集中注意力於）及 **one thing**

at a time（一次一件事），其次要知道頻率副詞（usually）
要放在動詞之前或 be 動詞之後，最後用五大句型之第三
型：S + V + O 即可解題。

14. She _____.

teacher / most / English / the / popular / at / school / is

答案： She is the most popular English teacher at school.

中譯： 她是學校最受歡迎的英文老師。

解析： 從關鍵字 **the, most, popular**（最受歡迎的）得知此題考
形容詞最高級的用法，其句型如下：
S + be + the + most + Adj（三音節及以上）**(+ N)...**
① He is the most interesting student in his class.
他是他班上最有趣的學生。
② She is the tallest of the three (girls).
她是三個人（女孩）當中最高的。

15. What _____!

smart / he / a / is / boy

答案： What a smart boy he is!

中譯： 他是個多麼聰明的孩子啊！

解析： 從句首 **What** 及句尾驚嘆號（!）得知此題考感嘆句的用
法，其句型如下：
What + a + Adj + N + S + be!
= How + Adj + a + N + S + be!
What a cute girl she is!
= How cute a girl she is!
= How cute she is/the girl is!
她是個多麼可愛的女孩啊！

第二部分　段落寫作

請依照題目要求,寫一篇約 50 字的段落。本部分採整體式評分
(0~5 級分),再轉換成百分制。評分要點包括重點表達的完整
性、文法、用字、拼字、字母大小寫、標點符號。

題目:
**昨天你在路上看到一起交通事故,請根據圖片寫一篇約 50
字的短文,來描述你所看到事件的經過。**

參考範文：

On my way home yesterday, I saw a fast motorcycle following a taxi very closely. Suddenly, the taxi stopped, and the motorcycle hit the taxi. The motorcyclist fell to the ground and was badly hurt. He cried out in pain. Soon the police officers came to deal with the accident, and the motorcyclist was sent to the hospital in an ambulance.

中譯：

　　昨天在回家的路上，我看見一部急駛的摩托車緊跟在一部計程車後面。突然間，計程車停了下來，摩托車便撞了上去。機車騎士摔倒在地上，傷勢嚴重。他痛苦地哀嚎。不久，警察前來處理這場交通事故，而機車騎士也被救護車送往醫院治療。

解析：

(1) 第一句 "On my way home yesterday, I saw a fast motorcycle following a taxi very closely." 點出主題：車禍發生的原因。接著根據主題句發展短文，描述車禍發生的經過。最後以警方前來處理作結。

(2) 動詞時態用過去式，符合描述文的需求。

(3) 句型有變化：簡單句 "He cried out in pain."、複合句 "Suddenly, the taxi stopped, and the motorcycle hit the taxi." "The motorcyclist fell to the ground and was badly hurt." "Soon the police officers came to deal with the accident, and the motorcyclist was sent to the hospital in an ambulance." 及複句 "On my way home yesterday, I saw a fast motorcycle following a taxi very closely."。

重要單字片語：

on one's way home　在某人回家路上

motorcycle = motorbike = scooter　摩托車

closely　緊臨地；緊密地

suddenly = all of a sudden = all at once　突然地

motorcyclist　機車騎士

be badly hurt = badly injured　傷勢嚴重

cry out　大叫

in pain　痛苦的

the police　警方（後接複數動詞）

police officer　警察

deal with = handle　處理；應付

accident　意外，事故；車禍（= car accident）

hospital　醫院

ambulance　救護車

第二組

Part II   Practice Test 2

第一章 試題卷

1 閱讀能力測驗

本測驗分三部分，全為四選一之選擇題，共 35 題，作答時間 40 分鐘。

第一部分　詞彙和結構

本部分共 15 題，每題含一個空格。請就試題冊上 A、B、C、D 四個選項中選出最適合題意的字或詞，標示在答案紙上。

Questions 1～15

1. These shoes were made in France, _____?
   A. aren't they
   B. didn't they
   C. weren't they
   D. wasn't it

2. Please keep it a _____. I don't want anybody to know it.
   A. promise
   B. safety
   C. silence
   D. secret

3. I wouldn't lend him money if I _____ you.
   A. am
   B. were
   C. see
   D. saw

4. You're getting fatter and fatter, so you'd better go
_____ a diet.
   A. on
   B. at
   C. from
   D. with

5. The teacher _____ to the students how to do the
homework.
   A. apologized
   B. expected
   C. explained
   D. elected

6. The students stopped _____ as soon as the teacher
entered the classroom.
   A. talking
   B. to talk
   C. talk
   D. talked

7. I was _____ with the show last night.
   A. boring
   B. bored
   C. bore
   D. to bore

8. Don't follow that taxi too _____. It might stop any
minute.
   A. carefully
   B. nearly
   C. safely
   D. closely

9. I felt very _____ when I found that I didn't have enough money to pay the bill in the restaurant.
A. dangerous
B. independent
C. excited
D. embarrassed

10. Lisa never wears dresses that are out of _____.
A. fashion
B. attention
C. realization
D. patience

11. Nancy _____ six books since 2001, and she is working on her seventh.
A. has written
B. writes
C. wrote
D. has been writing

12. You look tired. Why don't you go and _____ a nap?
A. make
B. take
C. do
D. try

13. Why don't you start by introducing _____?
A. you
B. your
C. yourself
D. yours

14. Come to my house. I have _____ to tell you.
    A. something important
    B. important something
    C. anything important
    D. important anything

15. Some people care about what they eat, while _____ don't.
    A. the other
    B. others
    C. the others
    D. another

第二部分　段落填空

本部分共 10 題，包括二個段落，每個段落各含 5 個空格。請就試題冊上 A、B、C、D 四個選項中選出最適合題意的字或詞，標示在答案紙上。

Questions 16～20

Dear Brenda,

　　I'm a little sad today because I can't see my mom （16）Mother's Day. I miss her so much.

　　We can only talk on the phone 　（17）　 I study in England, and my mom lives in Taiwan. My dad 　（18）　 long ago, and my mom works on her farm alone. She's in her sixties but very healthy. （19） her free time, my mom goes swimming.

　　Usually I don't feel sad. In fact, I enjoy 　（20）　 on my own. Maybe it's just because it's Mother's Day. Well, hope your family are well.

Best wishes,
Derek

16. A. at
    B. in
    C. on
    D. with

17. A. if
    B. because
    C. when
    D. so

18. A. dies
    B. dead
    C. died
    D. is dead

19. A. On
    B. At
    C. From
    D. In

20. A. to be
    B. be
    C. being
    D. am

Questions 21～25

Simon loves his dog, Anita. He loves her long ears, brown eyes and big mouth. But most of （21）, he loves her nose, which makes her a special dog.

What's special about Anita's nose? She can smell things （22） other animals can't. With her special nose, Anita helps the police （23） missing people.

One afternoon, a police officer called Simon for help. "Can you and Anita come to 25 Laker Street? Danny Brown （24）. His parents are so worried. Can you both help us to find him?" asked the officer. "Sure, we're （25） the way," said Simon. In less than three hours, Anita found the lost boy, Danny. And of course she did it this time with her special nose, too.

21. A. everything
    B. others
    C. all
    D. anything

22. A. what
    B. where
    C. who
    D. that

23. A. find
    B. finds
    C. found
    D. finding

24. A. missed
    B. misses
    C. is missing
    D. is missed

25. A. in
    B. on
    C. under
    D. from

第三部分　閱讀理解

本部分共 10 題，包括數段短文，每段短文後有 1～3 個相關問題，請就試題冊上 A、B、C、D 四個選項中選出最適合者，標示在答案紙上。

Question 26

• Deep Water!　Watch Out! •

26. Where is one most likely to see this sign?
A. At a library.
B. At a bank.
C. At a mall.
D. At a pool.

Questions 27～28

MISSING BOY

Missing since March 10 from TaiMall. Named Kenny, aged 5, wearing a white T-shirt & blue shorts.

If you see him or know anything about him, please contact me as soon as possible.

My wife and I are very sad and want him back badly.

Call Kevin at 2361-3877

Reward if found.

27. Who wrote this ad?
   A. Kevin's wife.
   B. Kenny's dad.
   C. Kevin's mom.
   D. Kenny's mom.

28. What was the missing boy wearing?
   A. A blue T-shirt and white shorts.
   B. A Micky Mouse T-shirt and blue shorts.
   C. A white T-shirt and blue shorts.
   D. A Doraemon T-shirt and white shorts.

Questions 29~30

INTERNATIONAL FLIGHTS

DESTINATION	TIME
New York	11:10 am
Los Angeles	11:25 am
San Francisco	11:40 am
Chicago	11:00 am
London	11:55 am
Paris	12:10 pm
Tokyo	12:25 pm
Hong Kong	12:40 pm
Singapore	12:50 pm
Toronto	1:00 pm
Sydney	1:10 pm

29. Nina and Derek are flying to Paris. What time is their flight?
 A. 11:40 am.
 B. 11:55 am.
 C. 12:10 pm.
 D. 12:25 pm.

30. Flights are leaving for all of the following cities EXCEPT?
 A. Sydney.
 B. Paris.
 C. London.
 D. Boston.

Questions 31~32

Hertford House, located in Toronto, Canada, is a special school where students are free to choose what classes they take. There are about one hundred students, aged six to eighteen, and fifteen teachers. The school does not make students go to classes, and it's okay if students do not go to classes. Students usually study in class for five hours a day, four days a week.

Except for safety rules, the students are allowed to make all the rules of the school. Everyone should follow the rules, but it's okay if students don't. Besides, Hertford House asks parents to join the life of the school. Many parents teach classes or help with club activities or sports events in their free time.

65

31. What will happen if students do not attend classes or follow the school rules?
    A. Their parents will be fined.
    B. They will have to leave school.
    C. They will be punished.
    D. Nothing.

32. Which of the following statements is not true?
    A. Hertford House is in Canada.
    B. Hertford House students can make all the rules of the school.
    C. Many parents help with club activities in school.
    D. Hertford House students can take what classes they want.

Questions 33~35

Dear Mike,

Long time no see, how have you been?

I'm writing to ask for your advice. I met a girl at a party three months ago. Her name is Michelle. She is pretty and has a beautiful voice. I have to tell you that I like her very much. However, I have a problem now. I hope you can solve it for me.

As I said, Michelle is a pretty girl and has a beautiful voice. I feel proud to be with her. We have fun together all the time. So far Michelle and I have had nine or ten dates... movies, dinners, concerts. The problem is that I paid for everything, even the taxi. She didn't offer to pay for anything. Never. It isn't fair.

What should I do? Please help me.

Johnny

33. What is this letter mostly about?

    A. Asking for money.

    B. Making a date.

    C. Eating dates.

    D. Sharing a bill.

34. What's Johnny's problem?

    A. He is poor.

    B. He is too busy.

    C. He can't marry his girlfriend.

    D. His girlfriend never pays for their dates.

35. Which of the following statements is not true?

    A. Mike and Johnny haven't seen each other for a long
       time.

    B. Mike met Michelle at a party.

    C. Michelle has a beautiful voice.

    D. Johnny paid for every date with Michelle.

2 寫作能力測驗

第一部分　單句寫作

請將答案寫在寫作能力測驗答案紙對應的題號旁，如有拼字、標點、大小寫之錯誤，將予扣分。

第 1～5 題：句子改寫

> 請依題目之提示，將原句改寫成指定型式，並將改寫的句子完整地寫在答案卷上（包括提示之文字及標點符號）。

1. They have lived in Taipei for ten years.
   How long _____?

2. He is a factory worker.
   They _____.

3. Tim will go swimming tomorrow.
   Tim _____ yesterday.

4. To ride a motorcycle with one hand is dangerous.
   It is dangerous _____.

5. She said to me, "Don't listen to Michael."
   She told me _____.

第 6～10 題：句子合併

請依照題目指示，將兩句合併成一句，並將合併的句子完整地
寫在答案卷上（包括提示之文字及標點符號）。

6. We stayed at a hotel.
   The hotel was near a lake.（用 which）

   _____

7. Penny loves swimming.
   Her sister loves swimming, too.（用 so）

   _____

8. My father is a teacher.
   My mother is a teacher.（用 not only... but also...）

   _____

9. Jenny left the office.
   She didn't tell anyone.（用 without）

   _____

10. Bill went swimming.
    He didn't study for the test.（用 instead of）

   _____

第 11～15 題：重組

請將題目中所有提示字詞整合成一有意義的句子，並將重組的
句子完整地寫在答案卷上（包括提示之文字及標點符號）。答
案中必須使用所有提示字詞，且不能隨意增加字詞，否則不予
計分。

---

11. There _____.
    a / accidents / yesterday / few / were /car

12. Across _____.
    my house / a / from / city library / is

13. The _____.
    your mom / tasted / that / cake / made / great

14. Michael _____.
    playing / after school / with / computer games / enjoys
    / his friends

15. I _____.
    in / jogging / the park / lost / while / was / my wallet / I

第二部分　段落寫作

請依照題目要求，寫一篇約 50 字的段落。本部分採整體式評分
（0～5 級分），再轉換成百分制。評分要點包括重點表達的完整
性、文法、用字、拼字、字母大小寫、標點符號。

題目：
**現在是星期天的早晨，請根據圖片寫一篇約50字的短文，來
描述你所看到的景象。**

第二章 解析卷

1 閱讀能力測驗

> 本測驗分三部分,全為四選一之選擇題,共 35 題,作答時間
> 40 分鐘。

第一部分　詞彙和結構

本部分共 15 題,每題含一個空格。請就試題冊上 A、B、C、D 四
個選項中選出最適合題意的字或詞,標示在答案紙上。

Questions 1~15

1. These shoes were made in France, _____?
A. aren't they
B. didn't they
C. weren't they
D. wasn't it
答案:(C)
中譯:這鞋子是法國製的,不是嗎?
解析:此題考「附加問句」的用法,其句型如下:
　　　S + be..., be-n't + S?
　　　① You are from Canada, aren't you?
　　　　 你來自加拿大,不是嗎?
　　　② You were at the beach yesterday, weren't you?
　　　　 你昨天去海邊,不是嗎?
　　　另外,其他參考句型及例句如下:
　　　S + V, don't/doesn't + S?
　　　S + don't/doesn't + V原形, do/does + S?
　　　S + Aux（助動詞）+ V原形, Aux-n't + S?
　　　S + Aux-n't + V原形, + Aux + S?
　　　S + have/has + p.p., haven't/hasn't + S?
　　　S + haven't/hasn't + p.p., + have/has + S?

① You **like** English, **don't** you?
你喜歡英文，不是嗎？

② You **don't like** English, **do** you?
你不喜歡英文，是不是？

③ You **can** swim, **can't** you?
你會游泳，不是嗎？

You **can't** swim, **can** you?
你不會游泳，是不是？

④ You **have eaten** lunch, **haven't** you?
你已經吃過午飯了，不是嗎？

You **haven't eaten** lunch, **have** you?
你還沒有吃午餐，是不是？

2. **Please keep it a _____ . I don't want anybody to know it.**

   A. promise

   B. safety

   C. silence

   D. secret

   答案：（D）

   中譯：請保密，我不要任何人知道這件事。

   解析：此題考「用字」，由第二句 "I don't want anybody to
   know it." 得知說話者要對方為其保守祕密，所以答案應選
   D. Secret（祕密）。另外，從字的用法 keep it a，亦可消
   去選項 B. safety（安全）及 C. silence（安靜）。至於選項
   A. promise（承諾）雖符合單字用法，但不合「語意」。

3. **I wouldn't lend him money if I _____ you.**

   A. am

   B. were

   C. see

   D. saw

答案：（B）

中譯：如果我是你的話，我就不會把錢借給他了。

解析：此題考與「現在事實相反」之假設語氣，其句型為：

$$If + S + \left\{ \begin{array}{l} V過去式 \\ were \end{array} \right., S + \left\{ \begin{array}{l} would \\ could \\ might \\ should \end{array} \right. + V原形$$

① If I had enough money, I would buy a new computer.

= I would buy a new computer if I had enough money.

如果我（現在）有足夠的錢，我會去買一台新電腦。

② If I were you, I would call the police.

= I would call the police if I were you.

如果我是你的話，我會去報警。

根據上述，答案 D. saw 雖符合文法，但不合「語意」，所以答案只能選 B. were。

4. You're getting fatter and fatter, so you'd better go _____ a diet.

A. on

B. at

C. from

D. with

答案：（A）

中譯：你現在愈來愈胖了，所以最好要節食／減肥。

解析：此題考慣用語 go on a diet（減肥，節食）。

5. The teacher _____ to the students how to do the homework.

A. apologized

B. expected

C. explained

D. elected

答案：（C）

中譯：老師向學生們解釋如何寫作業。

解析：此題考「單字」用法：

A. apologized　道歉

B. expected　期望；預期

C. explained　解釋

D. elected　選舉

根據題意，此題應選 C. explained（解釋）。

6. The students stopped _____ as soon as the teacher entered the classroom.

A. talking

B. to talk

C. talk

D. talked

答案：（A）

中譯：老師一進教室，學生就停止講話。

解析：此題考 stop 的用法：

stop + V-ing　停止做…

stop + to + V原形　停下目前的動作而去做…

① They **stopped working** as soon as their boss went out.

老板一外出，他們就停止工作。

② They were talking happily, but as soon as the boss entered the office, they **stopped to work**.

他們當時聊得很愉快，但是當老闆一走進辦公室，他們就停止聊天而開始工作。

7. I was _____ with the show last night.

A. boring

B. bored

C. bore

D. to bore

答案：(B)

中譯：我覺得昨晚的表演很無聊。

解析：此題考「情緒動詞」的用法：

人 + be bored with + 事物

事物 + be boring to + 人

事物 + bore + 人

I was bored with the TV show.

= The TV show was boring to me.

= The TV show bored me.

這個電視節目很無聊。

其他情緒動詞的例句如下：

① I was surprised at the news.

   = The news was surprising to me.

   = The news surprised me.

   這消息令我感到驚訝。

② The teacher was not satisfied with John's report.

   = John's report was not satisfying/satisfactory to the teacher.

   = John's report did not satisfy the teacher.

   老師不滿意 John 的報告內容。

③ I'm interested in fishing.

   = Fishing is interesting to me.

   = Fishing interests me.

   我對釣魚有興趣。

④ We were excited about the ball game.

   = The ball game was exciting to us.

   = The ball game excited us.

   我們看球賽看得很過癮。

8. Don't follow that taxi too _____. It might stop any minute.

   A. carefully

   B. nearly

   C. safely

   D. closely

   答案：（D）

   中譯：不要跟那部計程車跟得太緊，它隨時可能停車。

   解析：此題考「單字」用法：

   　　　A. carefully　小心地，仔細地

   　　　B. nearly　幾乎

   　　　C. safely　安全地

   　　　D. closely　緊密地，接近地；親密地；嚴密地

   　　　根據上述，只有 D. closely 符合語意。

9. I felt very _____ when I found that I didn't have enough money to pay the bill in the restaurant.

   A. dangerous

   B. independent

   C. excited

   D. embarrassed

   答案：（D）

   中譯：當我發現沒有足夠的錢去付餐廳的帳單時，我覺得很糗。

   解析：此題考「單字」用法：

   　　　A. dangerous　危險的

   　　　B. independent　獨立的

   　　　C. excited　感到興奮的

   　　　D. embarrassed　感到困窘的，難為情的，很糗的

   　　　根據上述，只有 D. embarrassed （很糗的）符合語意。

10. Lisa never wears dresses that are out of _____.

A. fashion

B. attention

C. realization

D. patience

答案：（A）

中譯：Lisa 從不穿過時的服裝。

解析：此題考慣用語 **out of fashion**（不合時宜的，過時的，落伍的）。

    A. fashion   時尚

    B. attention   專注，注意

    C. realization   了解；實現

    D. patience   耐心

    ※ **out of fashion = out of date = old-fashioned**：過時的。

11. Nancy _____ six books since 2001, and she is working on her seventh.

A. has written

B. writes

C. wrote

D. has been writing

答案：（A）

中譯：Nancy 自從二〇〇一年以來，已經寫了六本書，目前她正在寫第七本書。

解析：此題考 **since** 的用法：

    S + have/has + p.p. + since + S + p.t.（動詞過去式）

    S + have/has + p.p. + since + 特定時間

    ① I have lived in Taipei since I was six.

      我從六歲開始就住在台北。

    ② Two years have passed since he left.

      他離開已經有兩年了。

    ③ He has worked here since 2000.

      他從西元二千年就在這裡工作了。

since 的其他句型參考如下：

S + have/has + been + V-ing + since + S + V過去式

（表示到目前還在持續進行中）

S + have/has + been + V-ing + since + 特定時間

（表示到目前還在持續進行中）

① Joe has been watching TV since 2:00 in the afternoon.

　Joe 從下午兩點就一直看電視看到現在。

② Betty has been playing the piano since she came home.

　Betty 從回家以後就一直彈鋼琴彈到現在。

此外，since 尚有下列兩種用法：

It + is/has been + 一段時間 + since + S + V過去式

S + have/has + p.p. + since + 一段時間 + ago

① It is/has been three years since Mary left Taiwan.

　Mary 離開台灣已有兩年之久。

② She has eaten nothing since two days ago.

　她已經兩天沒吃東西了。

12. You look tired. Why don't you go and _____ a nap?

　A. make

　B. take

　C. do

　D. try

答案：（B）

中譯：你看起來很累的樣子，為什麼不去小睡一下？

解析：此題考慣用語 take a nap（小睡片刻）。

13. Why don't you start by introducing _____?

　A. you

　B. your

　C. yourself

　D. yours

答案：（C）

中譯：你何不先從自我介紹開始呢？

解析：此題考「反身代名詞」的用法，只要本身是發出動作的接
　　　受者（即受詞），就必須用反身代名詞：I→myself（我自
　　　己）、you→yourself（你自己）、he→himself（他自
　　　己）、she→herself（她自己）、it→itself（它自己）、we
　　　→ourselves（我們自己）、you→yourselves（你們自
　　　己）、they→themselves（他們自己）

① He killed himself last night.
　他昨晚自殺。

② Monica cut herself just now.
　Monica 剛剛割傷自己。

③ Please tell me a little about yourself.
　請簡單自我介紹一下。

根據上述，答案應選 C. yourself。

14. **Come to my house. I have _____ to tell you.**
A. something important
B. important something
C. anything important
D. important anything

答案：（A）

中譯：來我家，我有重要的事情要告訴你。

解析：**something, anything, nothing, everything** 如以「形容
　　　詞」修飾，則形容詞須置其「後」，即「後位修飾」，所以
　　　此題答案應選 A. something important（重要的事）。另外
　　　anything 用在「否定句」及「疑問句」，所以 C. anything
　　　important 不合文法。

15. Some people care about what they eat, while _____ don't.

A. the other

B. others

C. the others

D. another

答案：（B）

中譯：有些人在乎他們所吃的東西，而有些人則不在乎。

解析：此題考「代名詞」的用法：

A. the other　指剩下的唯一一人或物

I have two brothers. One is a doctor, and the other is a teacher.

我有兩個兄弟，一個是醫生，另一個是老師。

B. others　指其他的人、事、物（對象並不確定）

Some like skiing; others like skating.

有些人喜歡滑雪，有些人則喜歡溜冰。

C. the others　指剩下的人、事、物，為複數形

I have five brothers. One is a doctor, and the others are teachers.

我有五個兄弟，其中一個是醫生，其他（四個）都是老師。

D. another　另一個，可當形容詞及名詞

① I have three sisters. One is a nurse, another is a secretary, and the other is a student.

我有三個姊妹。一個是護士，另一個是祕書，還有一個是學生。

② I don't like this watch. Please show me another one.

我不喜歡這隻錶，請拿另一隻給我看看。

第二部分　段落填空

本部分共 10 題，包括二個段落，每個段落各含 5 個空格。請就試題冊上 A、B、C、D 四個選項中選出最適合題意的字或詞，標示在答案紙上。

Questions 16~20

Dear Brenda,

　　I'm a little sad today because I can't see my mom （16） Mother's Day. I miss her so much.

　　We can only talk on the phone （17） I study in England, and my mom lives in Taiwan. My dad （18） long ago, and my mom works on her farm alone. She's in her sixties but very healthy. （19） her free time, my mom goes swimming.

　　Usually I don't feel sad. In fact, I enjoy （20） on my own. Maybe it's just because it's Mother's Day. Well, hope your family are well.

　　　　　　　　　　　　　　　Best wishes,

　　　　　　　　　　　　　　　Derek

16. A. at
    B. in
    C. on
    D. with

17. A. if
    B. because
    C. when
    D. so

18. A. dies
    B. dead
    C. died
    D. is dead

19. A. On
    B. At
    C. From
    D. In

20. A. to be
    B. be
    C. being
    D. am

答案：16.（C） 17.（B） 18.（C） 19.（D） 20.（C）

中譯：

親愛的 Brenda:

　　我今天有點難過，因為我無法在母親節當天見到我媽媽。我很想她。

　　我們只能通電話，原因是我在英國求學，而我媽住在台灣。我父親很久以前就過世了，而我母親則獨自在農場工作。她今年六十幾歲，不過身體還蠻健康的。有空的時候，我媽會去游泳。

　　通常我都不會感到難過。事實上，我蠻喜歡獨立的感覺。也許是因為遇到母親節的緣故吧！嗯，希望你的家人都很健康。

獻上最佳祝福
Derek

解析：

16. 「特定節日、星期或特殊日子」介詞須用 **on**，如 **on** Mother's Day, **on** Christmas, **on** my birthday, **on** their 10th wedding anniversary（在他們的結婚十週年慶）, **on** this unforgettable day（在這個難忘的日子）, **on** Sunday, **on** weekends 等。

17. A. if　假如
    B. because　因為
    C. when　當
    D. so　所以
    由語意得知，本題考的是「因果關係」，所以答案應選 B. because（因為）。

18. 由 **... long ago** 得知空格應填「動詞過去式」，所以答案應選 C. died。

19. **in one's free time**（在某人空閒之時）
    I play basketball in my free time.
    = I play basketball when/whenever I'm free.
    我有空時就打籃球。

20. **enjoy + V-ing/N**
    ① I enjoy getting up late on Sundays.
      我喜歡星期天晚起／賴床。
    ② We enjoyed the dinner very much.
      我們晚餐吃得很愉快。

Question 21~25

Simon loves his dog, Anita. He loves her long ears, brown eyes and big mouth. But most of __(21)__, he loves her nose, which makes her a special dog.

What's special about Anita's nose? She can smell things __(22)__ other animals can't. With her special nose, Anita helps the police __(23)__ missing people.

One afternoon, a police officer called Simon for help. "Can you and Anita come to 25 Laker Street? Danny Brown __(24)__. His parents are so worried. Can you both help us to find him?" asked the officer. "Sure, we're __(25)__ the way," said Simon. In less than three hours, Anita found the lost boy, Danny. And of course she did it this time with her special nose, too.

21. A. everything
    B. others
    C. all
    D. anything

22. A. what
    B. where
    C. who
    D. that

23. A. find
    B. finds
    C. found
    D. finding

24. A. missed
    B. misses
    C. is missing
    D. is missed

25. A. in
    B. on
    C. under
    D. from

答案：21.（C）　22.（D）　23.（A）　24.（C）　25.（B）

中譯：

> 　　Simon 很愛他的狗 Anita，他愛牠的長耳朵、棕眼及大嘴巴。他尤其喜愛牠的鼻子，那也使 Anita 成為一隻特殊的狗。
>
> 　　Anita 的鼻子有何特殊呢？牠可以嗅到其他動物沒有辦法嗅到的東西。靠著牠特殊的鼻子，Anita 協助警方尋找失蹤人口。
>
> 　　有一天下午，一名警察打電話向 Simon 求助。「你跟 Anita 可以來 Laker 街 25 號這裡嗎？Danny Brown 失蹤了，他的父母十分擔心。你倆可以幫我們找到他嗎？」警察問道。「沒問題，我們馬上過去。」Simon 說道。不到三小時的時間，Anita 就找到失蹤的男孩 Danny。當然，這次牠也是靠著牠那特殊的鼻子辦到的。

解析：

21. most of all：尤其，特別。

22. 此題考「關係代名詞」的用法：

    A. what：指「…的人、事、物」（= the one(s) that; the thing(s) that）

    B. where：先行詞為「地方」（= in which）

    C. who：先行詞為「人」

    D. that：先行詞為「人、事、物、受格或時間」（= who, which, whom, when）

    ① This is what we want.

      這是我們所要的。

    ② Jane is not what she was.

      = Jane is not what she used to be.

      Jane 已經不是以前的她了。

③ The house where Judy lives is beautiful.

= The house in which Judy lives is beautiful.

Judy 住的那棟房子很漂亮。

④ The man who lives above us is not nice.

住在我們樓上的那個男的不友善。

⑤ She can do things that other girls can't.

她會做一些其他女孩子不會做的事情。

由於題目的先行詞為 **things**，所以「關係代名詞」只能選 D. that
（= which）。

23. 此題考 help 的用法：

help + 受詞 + **to** + **V**原形

help + 受詞 + **V**原形

help + 受詞 + **with** + 事物

Please help me **to carry** the bag.

= Please help me **carry** the bag.

= Please help me **with** the bag.

請幫我提行李／包包。

24. A. missed　錯過；思念

B. misses　錯過；思念

C. is missing　失蹤的

D. is missed　被錯過，被思念

根據上下文，只有選項 C. is missing 符合語意。

25. 此題考「片語」用法：

in one's way　擋路

on one's/the way　在路上；馬上來

under way　進行中

① You're in my way.

你擋到我的路了。

② I saw an accident on my/the way **to** school.

上學途中，我看見一場意外。

I ran into my teacher on my/the way home.

回家途中，我撞見我的老師。

③ The plan is under way.

計畫在進行中。

根據 way 的片語用法，即可消去 C. under 及 D. from（因為沒有意義）。而根據上下文，又可消去 A. in（因不合語意），所以答案只能選 B. on。另外，Sure, we're on the way. 亦可寫成：Sure, we'll be on the way.（沒問題，馬上過去。）

第三部分　閱讀理解

本部分共 10 題，包括數段短文，每段短文後有 1～3 個相關問題，請就試題冊上 A、B、C、D 四個選項中選出最適合者，標示在答案紙上。

Question 26

• **Deep Water!　Watch Out!** •

26. Where is one most likely to see this sign?
   A. At a library.
   B. At a bank.
   C. At a mall.
   D. At a pool.

第 26 題

• 水　深　！　小　心　！ •

26. 題目：在哪裡最可能看到這個告示牌？
   選項：A. 在圖書館。
   　　　B. 在銀行。
   　　　C. 在購物中心。
   　　　D. 在游泳池。
   答案：（D）

Questions 27~28

MISSING BOY

Missing since March 10 from TaiMall. Named Kenny, aged 5, wearing a white T-shirt & blue shorts.

If you see him or know anything about him, please contact me as soon as possible.

My wife and I are very sad and want him back badly.

Call Kevin at 2361-3877

Reward if found.

27. Who wrote this ad?
    A. Kevin's wife.
    B. Kenny's dad.
    C. Kevin's mom.
    D. Kenny's mom.

28. What was the missing boy wearing?
    A. A blue T-shirt and white shorts.
    B. A Micky Mouse T-shirt and blue shorts.
    C. A white T-shirt and blue shorts.
    D. A Doraemon T-shirt and white shorts.

第 27～28 題

失蹤男童

　　自從三月十號在台茂（購物中心）走失至今。男孩名叫 Kenny，今年五歲，失蹤當天身穿白 T 恤及藍短褲。

　　如果您看到這個男童，或有任何關於他的消息，請儘快跟我聯絡。

　　我和我太太非常傷心，望子心切。

　　請打 2361-3877 與 Kevin 聯繫。

　　尋獲有賞。

---

27. 題目：何人寫這則廣告？

　　選項：A. Kevin 的太太。

　　　　　B. Kenny 的爸爸。

　　　　　C. Kevin 的媽媽。

　　　　　D. Kenny 的媽媽。

　　答案：（B）

28. 題目：失蹤男童的穿著為何？

　　選項：A. 藍 T 恤及白短褲。

　　　　　B. 印有米老鼠的 T 恤及藍短褲。

　　　　　C. 白 T 恤及藍短褲。

　　　　　D. 印有哆啦 A 夢的 T 恤及白短褲。

　　答案：（C）

Questions 29~30

INTERNATIONAL FLIGHTS

DESTINATION	TIME
New York	11:10 am
Los Angeles	11:25 am
San Francisco	11:40 am
Chicago	11:00 am
London	11:55 am
Paris	12:10 pm
Tokyo	12:25 pm
Hong Kong	12:40 pm
Singapore	12:50 pm
Toronto	1:00 pm
Sydney	1:10 pm

29. **Nina and Derek are flying to Paris. What time is their flight?**
    A. 11:40 am.
    B. 11:55 am.
    C. 12:10 pm.
    D. 12:25 pm.

30. **Flights are leaving for all of the following cities EXCEPT?**
    A. Sydney.
    B. Paris.
    C. London.
    D. Boston.

第 29～30 題

```
          國  際  航  班

    抵達地點              時  間
    紐  約              早上 11:10
    洛杉磯              早上 11:25
    舊金山              早上 11:40
    芝加哥              早上 11:00
    倫  敦              早上 11:55
    巴  黎              中午 12:10
    東  京              中午 12:25
    香  港              中午 12:40
    新加坡              中午 12:50
    多倫多              下午  1:00
    雪  梨              下午  1:10
```

29. 題目： Nina 和 Derek 要搭機前往巴黎，他們的班機是幾點？
    選項： A. 早上十一點四十分。

    　　　 B. 早上十一點五十五分。

    　　　 C. 中午十二點十分。

    　　　 D. 中午十二點二十五分。

    答案：（C）

30. 題目： 下列哪個城市沒有班機抵達？
    選項： A. 雪梨。

    　　　 B. 巴黎。

    　　　 C. 倫敦。

    　　　 D. 波士頓。

    答案：（D）

Questions 31~32

> Hertford House, located in Toronto, Canada, is a special school where students are free to choose what classes they take. There are about one hundred students, aged six to eighteen, and fifteen teachers. The school does not make students go to classes, and it's okay if students do not go to classes. Students usually study in class for five hours a day, four days a week.
>
> Except for safety rules, the students are allowed to make all the rules of the school. Everyone should follow the rules, but it's okay if students don't. Besides, Hertford House asks parents to join the life of the school. Many parents teach classes or help with club activities or sports events in their free time.

31. What will happen if students do not attend classes or follow the school rules?
    A. Their parents will be fined.
    B. They will have to leave school.
    C. They will be punished.
    D. Nothing.

32. Which of the following statements is not true?
    A. Hertford House is in Canada.
    B. Hertford House students can make all the rules of the school.
    C. Many parents help with club activities in school.
    D. Hertford House students can take what classes they want.

第 31～32 題

> 位於加拿大多倫多的 Hertford House 是一所很特別的學校。那裡的學生可以自由選課。該校約有一百名學生（年齡六至十八歲不等）和十五位教師。學校並沒有硬性規定學生要去上課，如果學生不去上課，也沒關係。學生通常一週上課四天，每天五個小時。
>
> 　除了安全守則之外，學生可以自定所有的校規。每個人都應遵守校規，但是如果學生不遵守的話，也不會有事。此外，Hertford House 要求家長參與學校活動。很多家長選擇在空閒的時候到學校教課或協助社團活動及運動項目。

31. 題目： 如果學生不去上課或違反校規的話，那會怎麼樣？
    選項： A. 他們的父母會被罰款。
    　　　 B. 他們必須休學。
    　　　 C. 他們會被處罰。
    　　　 D. 不會怎麼樣。
    答案：（D）

32. 題目： 以下何者為非？
    選項： A. Hertford House 位於加拿大。
    　　　 B. Hertford House 的學生可以制定所有的校規。
    　　　 C. 很多家長協助學校的社團活動。
    　　　 D. Hertford House 的學生可以自由選課。
    答案：（B）

Questions 33~35

> Dear Mike,
>
> Long time no see, how have you been?
>
> I'm writing to ask for your advice. I met a girl at a party three months ago. Her name is Michelle. She is pretty and has a beautiful voice. I have to tell you that I like her very much. However, I have a problem now. I hope you can solve it for me.
>
> As I said, Michelle is a pretty girl and has a beautiful voice. I feel proud to be with her. We have fun together all the time. So far Michelle and I have had nine or ten dates... movies, dinners, concerts. The problem is that I paid for everything, even the taxi. She didn't offer to pay for anything. Never. It isn't fair.
>
> What should I do? Please help me.
>
> *Johnny*

33. What is this letter mostly about?
    A. Asking for money.
    B. Making a date.
    C. Eating dates.
    D. Sharing a bill.

34. What's Johnny's problem?
    A. He is poor.
    B. He is too busy.
    C. He can't marry his girlfriend.
    D. His girlfriend never pays for their dates.

35. Which of the following statements is not true?
    A. Mike and Johnny haven't seen each other for a long
       time.
    B. Mike met Michelle at a party.
    C. Michelle has a beautiful voice.
    D. Johnny paid for every date with Michelle.

第 33～35 題

親愛的 Mike,
　　好久不見，近來可好？
　　我寫信是要尋求你的建議。三個月前，我在派對上認識了
一個女生，她叫作 Michelle，人長得漂亮，而且聲音很美。我
必須告訴你我很喜歡她。然而，我現在有一個問題，希望你能
幫我解決。
　　如同我所說的，Michelle 人長得漂亮，而且聲音很好聽，
跟她在一起讓我感到很驕傲。我們在一起時總是那麼樣的開
心。到目前為止，我們約會已有九次、十次之多，像是看電
影、吃飯、聽音樂會。問題是每次都是我付帳，就連搭計程車
也是。她都沒有主動表示過要付帳，從來沒有！這不公平。
　　我該怎麼辦？請幫幫我。

Johnny

33. 題目：這封信的主旨為何？（這封信主要在探討什麼？）
　　選項：A. 要錢。
　　　　　B. 安排約會。
　　　　　C. 吃棗子。
　　　　　D. 分攤帳單。
　　答案：（D）

34. 題目：Johnny 的問題是什麼？

    選項：A. 他沒錢。（他很窮。）

    　　　B. 他太忙。

    　　　C. 他無法娶他的女友。

    　　　D. 約會時，他的女友從未付過帳。

    答案：（D）

35. 題目：下列何者為非？

    選項：A. Mike 和 Johnny 很久沒有碰面。

    　　　B. Mike 在派對上遇到 Michelle。

    　　　C. Michelle 的聲音很美。

    　　　D. 每次跟 Michelle 約會都是 Johnny 買單。

    答案：（B）

2 寫作能力測驗

請將答案寫在寫作能力測驗答案紙對應的題號旁，如有拼字、標點、大小寫之錯誤，將予扣分。

第 1～5 題：句子改寫

> 請依題目之提示，將原句改寫成指定型式，並將改寫的句子完整地寫在答案卷上（包括提示之文字及標點符號）。

1. **They have lived in Taipei for ten years.**
   How long _____?

   答案：How long **have they lived in Taipei?**

   中譯：他們在台北住了多久？

   解析：此題考 **How long** 的用法，其句型如下：
   How long have/has + S + p.p.?
   How long have/has + S + been + V-ing?

   ① A: How long have you lived in Taipei?
   B: For ten years.
   A：你在台北住了多久？
   B：十年。

   ② A: How long have you been working in this company?
   B: Since 1998.
   A：你在這家公司工作了多久？
   B：從一九九八年開始。

   ③ A: How long have you been here?
   B: I've been here for two years.
   A：你在這裡待了多久？
   B：我在這裡待了兩年。

2. He is a factory worker.

They _____.

答案： They **are factory workers**.

中譯： 他們是工廠工人／作業員。

解析： 此題考單複數互換的概念，其規則如下：

代名詞：
- he/she/it → they
- you → you
- I → we

be 動詞：
- am/is → are
- was → were

動詞：V-s → V

① It is a cute dog.

　　→ They are cute dogs.

② He was at the beach yesterday.

　　→ They were at the beach yesterday.

③ She lives in Canada.

　　→ They live in Canada.

※ 相關句子請參考姊妹作《全民英檢初級保證班》「寫作題型全都錄」。

3. Tim will go swimming tomorrow.

Tim _____ **yesterday.**

答案： Tim **went swimming** yesterday.

中譯： Tim 昨天去游泳。

解析： 由句尾 **yesterday** 得知此題考時態過去式的用法，其句型如下：

S + V過去式

I went shopping with my mom yesterday.

我昨天跟我媽去逛街。

4. To ride a motorcycle with one hand is dangerous.

It is dangerous _____.

答案：It is dangerous **to ride a motorcycle with one hand.**

中譯：單手騎機車很危險。

解析：此題考慮／假主詞與不定詞的互換句型：

To + V + is + Adj/N

= It is + Adj/N + to + V

① To swim alone in the river is dangerous.

= It is dangerous to swim alone in the river.

一個人在河裡游泳很危險。

② It is lots of fun to learn English songs.

= To learn English songs is lots of fun.

學英文歌很好玩。

上述句子亦可寫成動名詞形式：

① **Swimming** alone in the river is dangerous.

= It is dangerous **swimming** alone in the river.

② **Learning** English songs is lots of fun.

= It is lots of fun **learning** English songs.

5. She said to me, "Don't listen to Michael."

She told me _____.

答案：She told me **not to listen to Michael.**

中譯：她告訴我不要聽 Michael 的話。

解析：此題考直接敘述轉化成 tell 的用法，其句型如下：

S + tell + O + to + V原形

① I told you to be on time.

我告訴你要準時的。

② She told me not to phone you.

她告訴我不要打電話給你。

S + tell + O + that + S + V

S + tell + I.O.（間接受詞）**+ D.O.**（直接受詞）

① I'll tell him that you called.
我會告訴他你來電。
② She told me this.
她告訴我這件事。

※ 直接敘述與間接敘述的用法請參考姊妹作《全民英檢初級
保證班》「文法要點 12」名詞子句及「寫作題型全都錄」。

第 6～10 題：句子合併

請依照題目指示，將兩句合併成一句，並將合併的句子完整地
寫在答案卷上（包括提示之文字及標點符號）。

6. We stayed at a hotel.
The hotel was near a lake.（用 which）

_____.

答案：We stayed at a hotel which was near a lake.
中譯：我們住在一個靠近湖泊的旅館。
解析：此題考形容詞子句的用法。由於先行詞為 a hotel，屬於
事物，所以關係代名詞須用 which。
獨立子句為：We stayed at a hotel.
附屬子句為形容詞子句：which was near a lake.
關係代名詞 which 當形容詞子句的主詞。在此合併成複句
（complex sentence）"We stayed at a hotel which was
near a lake." 這裡的 which was 可以省略，亦即答案可簡
化為：We stayed at a hotel near a lake. 但底下例句則不
可：
We stayed at a hotel which was cheap but good.
我們住在一家便宜但很好的旅館。

但若執意要去掉 which was，則上句須改成：

We stayed at a cheap but good hotel.

不過這就成了簡單句（simple sentence）或五大基本句型的第三式：**S + V + O**。

※ 形容詞子句及四大變化句型的用法可參考姊妹作《全民英檢初級保證班》「文法要點 **12**」子句及「段落寫作 **2**」段落文章必殺句型。

7. Penny loves swimming.
Her sister loves swimming, too.（用 so）

_____.

答案：Penny loves swimming, and so does her sister.

中譯：Penny 很喜歡游泳，而她姊妹也是。

解析：此句亦等於：Penny loves swimming, and her sister does, too.

此題考 so（也）的用法，其句型如下：

S1 + V, and so + do/does + S2

S1 + V過去式, and so + did + S2

S1 + be..., and so + be + S2

S1 + be過去式..., and so + be過去式 + S2

S1 + Aux（助動詞）+ V原形, and so + Aux + S2

① Jenny loves cooking, and so do I.
　Jenny 喜愛做菜，而我也是。

② Tom went swimming yesterday, and so did we.
　Tom 昨天去游泳，而我們也是。

③ Nina is a great cook, and so is her mom.
　Nina 很會做菜，而她媽媽也是。

④ Lenny and Jack were at the museum yesterday, and so was I.
　Lenny 和 Jack 昨天去博物館，而我也是。

⑤ Judy can dance, and so can I.
　Judy 會跳舞，而我也會。

8. My father is a teacher.

　　My mother is a teacher.（用 not only... but also...）

_____ .

答案：Not only my father but also my mother is a teacher.

中譯：不只我爸爸，連我媽媽也是老師。

解析：此題考 **not only... but also...** 的用法，其句型如下：

Not only + S1 + but also + S2 + V

S + V + not only + A + but also + B

S + be + not only + A + but also + B

Not only + be + S + C（補語），but + S + be + also + C

Not only + Aux（助動詞） + S + V原形, but S + Aux + also + V

① Not only Jack but also his sisters **are** hard-working.

　　不只是 Jack，連他的姊妹們都很勤奮。

② He loves not only Landy but also Sally.

　　他不只愛 Landy，還愛 Sally。

③ Nina is not only pretty but also smart.

　　Nina 不但人漂亮，而且也很聰明。

④ Not only **was** she angry, but she was also worried.

　　她不但生氣，而且也滿擔心的。

⑤ Not only **can** he fix the car, but he can also cook.

　　他不會會修車，而且還會做菜。

⑥ Not only **did** he go to Japan, but he also dated a Japanese girl.

　　他不但去了日本，而且還跟日本女孩約會。

※ 第四、五句型及例句 ④ ～ ⑥ 皆為倒裝用法。

9. Jenny left the office.

　　She didn't tell anyone.（用 without）

_____ .

答案：Jenny left the office without telling anyone.

中譯：Jenny離開公司沒有告訴任何人。
解析：此題考 without（沒有）的用法，其句型如下：
S + V + without + V-ing
S + V + without + N
① He left without saying good-bye.
他不告而別。
② I usually go to school without breakfast.
我通常不吃早餐就去上學。

10. Bill went swimming.
He didn't study for the test.（用 instead of）

_____.

答案：Bill went swimming instead of studying for the test.
＝ Instead of studying for the test, Bill went swimming.
中譯：Bill 去游泳而沒有準備考試。
解析：此題考 instead of 的用法，其句型如下：
S + V + instead of + V-ing/N
Instead of + V-ing/N, S + V
① She went shopping instead of doing her homework.
＝Instead of doing her homework, she went shopping.
她去逛街而沒有寫功課。
② I'll have beef instead of pork.
＝Instead of pork, I'll have beef.
我要牛肉而不要豬肉。

第 11～15 題：重組

請將題目中所有提示字詞整合成一有意義的句子，並將重組的
句子完整地寫在答案卷上（包括提示之文字及標點符號）。答
案中必須使用所有提示字詞，且不能隨意增加字詞，否則不予
計分。

11. There _____.

a / accidents / yesterday / few / were /car

答案：There **were a few car accidents yesterday**.

中譯：昨天有幾起交通事故。

解析：此題考 There are 及過去式的用法，其句型如下：

There are + 複數名詞**...**（表現在）

There were + 複數名詞**...**（表過去）

There will be + 單／複數名詞**...**（表未來）

① There are five people in my family.
我家裡有五個人。

② There were many tourists here last night.
昨晚這裡有很多觀光客。

③ There will be a typhoon on Monday.
禮拜一將會有颱風。

※ There is a mouse in the house.
房子裡有一隻老鼠。

There was an earthquake last weekend.
上週末發生地震。

12. Across _____.

my house / a / from / city library / is

答案：Across **from my house is a city library**.

中譯：我住家的對面是市立圖書館。

解析：此題考倒裝句的用法，其句型如下：

Across from + N + be + N   在…的對面是…

Next to + N + be + N   在…的隔壁是…

Between + A + and + B + be + N   在 A 與 B 的中間是…

Here + be + N

Here + V + N

Here + Pron.（代名詞）+ V

① Across from my house is a bank.
= A bank is across from my house.
我房子的對面是銀行。

② Next to the school is a convenience store.

= A convenience store is next to the school.

學校的隔壁是一家便利商店。

③ Between the bank and the supermarket is a bakery.

= A bakery is between the bank and the supermarket.

銀行和超市的中間是麵包店。

④ Here is your change.

這是你的零錢。

⑤ Here comes the bus.

公車來了。

⑥ Here he comes.

他來了。

⑦ Here you are.

拿去／到了。

13. The _____.

your mom / tasted / that / cake / made / great

答案：The **cake that your mom made tasted great**.

中譯：你媽媽做的蛋糕嚐起來很棒／很好吃。

解析：此題考形容詞子句及連綴動詞的用法，其句型如下：

S + that + S + V + 連綴V + C（補語）

① The girl that you dated last night looked great.

你昨天約會的那個女孩滿好看的。

② The joke that you told sounded good.

你說的笑話聽起來還滿不錯的。

③ The flowers that you bought last time smelled good.

你上次買的花很香。

④ The shirt that you gave me felt great.

你送我的那件襯衫觸感很好。

⑤ The food that you cooked tasted great.

你做的菜很好吃。

※ **that** 在此皆可省略（因為當受詞用）。

14. Michael _____.

playing / after school / with / computer games / enjoys / his friends

答案：Michael enjoys playing computer games with his friends after school.

中譯：Michael 喜歡放學後跟朋友玩電腦遊戲。

解析：此題考 enjoy 的用法，其後接 V-ing 或 N。所以先找出 V-ing（playing），再找搭配詞（computergames, after school），最後再把介系詞（with）及其後之受詞（名詞，his friends）找出，句子便完成了。當然，要運用五大基本句型之第三型：S + V + O 來協助構句。

15. I _____.

in / jogging / the park / lost / while / was / my wallet / I

答案：I lost my wallet while I was jogging in the park.

中譯：我在公園慢跑時，掉了皮夾。

解析：此句亦可寫成：

While I was jogging in the park, I lost my wallet.

= Jogging in the park, I lost my wallet.

此題考含 while 的過去進行式的用法，其句型如下：

S + V過去式 + while + S + was/were + V-ing

While + S + was/were + V-ing, S + V過去式

The fire broke out while he was sleeping upstairs.

= While he was sleeping upstairs, the fire broke out.

大火發生時，他正在樓上睡覺。

上句亦可寫成：

He was sleeping upstairs when the fire broke out.

= When the fire broke out, he was sleeping upstairs.

第二部分　段落寫作

請依照題目要求,寫一篇約 50 字的段落。本部分採整體式評分
(0~5 級分),再轉換成百分制。評分要點包括重點表達的完整
性、文法、用字、拼字、字母大小寫、標點符號。

題目:
現在是星期天的早晨,請根據圖片寫一篇約50字的短文,來
描述你所看到的景象。

參考範文：

    It is a Sunday morning, and there are a lot of people in the park. Some are taking a walk, some are chatting, some are playing ball, some are dancing, some are walking their dogs, and some are reading. It is a sunny day, and it is good for people to spend a Sunday morning in a park.

中譯：

    這是星期天的早晨，公園裡有許多人。有些人在散步，有些人在聊天，有些人在打球，有些人在跳舞，有些人在遛狗，而有些人在看書。這是個晴空萬里的日子，也是人們在公園裡消磨週日早晨的好時光。

解析：

(1) 第一句 "It is a Sunday morning, and there are a lot of people in the park." 點出本文的主題：熱鬧的晨間公園。

(2) 接著根據主題描述多樣的公園活動。

(3) 時態用現在簡單式及現在進行式，符合描寫文的時態需要。

(4) 結尾點出週日早晨天氣晴朗，極適合人們到公園消磨時間，前後呼應，一氣呵成。

第三組

Part III

Practice Test 3

第一章 試題卷

1 閱讀能力測驗

本測驗分三部分，全為四選一之選擇題，共 35 題，作答時間
40 分鐘。

第一部分　詞彙和結構

本部分共 15 題，每題含一個空格。請就試題冊上 A、B、C、D 四
個選項中選出最適合題意的字或詞，標示在答案紙上。

Questions 1～15

1. It's pretty _____ to go hiking in such bad weather.
   A. safe
   B. social
   C. talkative
   D. dangerous

2. This restaurant _____ people. Let's try some others.
   A. is afraid of
   B. is full of
   C. is aware of
   D. is out of

3. Ben looks smart, but not as _____ as his brother.
   A. clever
   B. more clever
   C. most clever
   D. less clever

4. Kenny is _____ man I've ever seen.

 A. an interesting

 B. a more interesting

 C. the most interesting

 D. a less interesting

5. Let's ask Johnny _____ yesterday.

 A. what does the teacher say

 B. what did the teacher say

 C. what the teacher says

 D. what the teacher said

6. Everybody knows _____ Michael Jordan is a famous basketball player.

 A. what

 B. that

 C. how

 D. when

7. Please _____ your brother while I'm away.

 A. take care of

 B. take part in

 C. get rid of

 D. run out of

8. Derek never misses a single NBA game. He _____ be a basketball fan.

 A. can't

 B. couldn't

 C. must

 D. will

9. If it rains tomorrow, the game will have to _____.
   A. cancel
   B. cancels
   C. canceling
   D. be canceled

10. Can anyone help me _____ this bag? It's too heavy for me.
    A. carry
    B. carrying
    C. carried
    D. carries

11. _____ you home alone when I called you yesterday?
    A. Do
    B. Did
    C. Were
    D. Are

12. Kevin failed the English test. He _____ harder last week.
    A. should study
    B. should have studied
    C. must study
    D. must have studied hard

13. An _____ will be held in the new park tonight.
    A. outdoors concert
    B. concert outdoors
    C. outdoor concert
    D. concert outdoor

14. It's not easy for anyone to fall _____ in Mr. Wang's
class. He is so funny.
A. sleep
B. sleeping
C. asleep
D. slept

15. My computer works better and faster than _____.
A. you
B. her
C. its
D. his

第二部分　段落填空

本部分共 10 題，包括二個段落，每個段落各含 5 個空格。請就試題冊上 A、B、C、D 四個選項中選出最適合題意的字或詞，標示在答案紙上。

Questions 16～20

>   Michael and Jenny met at a party one night. For Michael, it was love ＿＿(16)＿＿ first sight, but not for Jenny. However, they talked ＿＿(17)＿＿ very late at night. When they left the party, it was almost 1 A.M. For the next three months, Michael and Jenny spent every weekend together. They went to the movies, museums, and restaurants together. One night at a nice restaurant, Michael asked Jenny ＿＿(18)＿＿ she would marry him, but she said no. The reason was that she was not ready to get married.
>
>   Michael was very sad, but he wouldn't ＿＿(19)＿＿. He began to write love letters to Jenny every day. In two years, Michael had sent Jenny about 700 love letters. At last, Jenny said, "I'm ready to get married now." To everyone's surprise, the one Jenny wanted to marry was not Michael ＿＿(20)＿＿ the mailman who had delivered his love letters to Jenny for two years. She said she began to fall in love with the mail carrier when he delivered Michael's 365th letter to her.

16. A. in
    B. at
    C. for
    D. on

17. A. before
    B. after
    C. once
    D. until

18. A. when
    B. that
    C. unless
    D. if

19. A. stay up
    B. give up
    C. make up
    D. look up

20. A. and
    B. or
    C. but
    D. however

Questions 21～25

Dear Nina,

Long time no see, how's everything? I haven't heard （21） you for a long time. I hope you're doing fine. I have good news （22） you. I have a ten-day vacation from next Friday. Would you like to come and stay with me? There are a lot of things to do and places to go.

I still remember the last time （23） you were here with me. We had great fun. Do you remember the day we went hiking on a cloudy day? We got lost in the mountains and were （24） . My parents called the police for help. When the police found us, we were so

cold and hungry __（25）__ we both could hardly move.
That was an unforgettable day.

Please let me know if you can come as soon as
possible. Say hello to your parents.

Love,

Lisa

21. A. of
    B. from
    C. with
    D. on

22. A. tell
    B. told
    C. telling
    D. to tell

23. A. which
    B. where
    C. when
    D. who

24. A. excited
    B. successful
    C. pleasant
    D. scared

25. A. that
    B. as
    C. until
    D. if

第三部分　閱讀理解

本部分共 10 題，包括數段短文，每段短文後有 1～3 個相關問題，請就試題冊上 A、B、C、D 四個選項中選出最適合者，標示在答案紙上。

Question 26

• **This Platform Is Not In Use** •

26. Where can you see this sign?
    A. In a park.
    B. In a meeting room.
    C. At the train station.
    D. At the airport.

Questions 27～28

ANDY'S WEAR & BOOTS
SUMMER SALE
August 21-31
50% off for T-shirts
40% off for shirts
60% off for shorts
30% off for boots
HURRY IN BEFORE IT'S TOO LATE

27. When does Andy's store have a sale?
    A. In June.
    B. In July.
    C. In August.
    D. In September.

28. If a T-shirt costs $300, how much will you have to pay
    for two T-shirts on sale?
    A. $150.
    B. $200.
    C. $250.
    D. $300.

Questions 29~30

WONDERLAND CAFE

Lunch Specials

◇ Steak, Potato & Salad   NT$180
◇ Fish, Potato & Salad   NT$150
◇ Chicken, Potato & Salad   NT$120
◇ Pork, Rice & Salad   NT$120

All meals served with bread & your choice of beverage.

29. If you order a chicken special, what will you get besides chicken?
    A. Potato, salad, cake, and tea.
    B. Salad, potato, bread, and coffee.
    C. Potato, salad, and juice.
    D. Salad, rice, and coffee.

30. How much will you have to pay if you and your friends order one steak special and two fish specials?
    A. NT$480.
    B. NT$360.
    C. NT$450.
    D. NT$390.

Questions 31~32

Last Saturday was Tina's birthday, but she was not happy at all. First, the weather was terrible. Then her pet dog was sick. What was worse, many of her friends did not go to her party. She felt very sad, angry and lonely. She cried, "It isn't fair."

However, the next day when she got to the classroom, she found a big box on her desk. She was surprised. It was from her classmates. There were cards, flowers, chocolates and presents in the box. Tina was very excited to see those things. It was a very unforgettable moment for her.

31. How did Tina feel when she found a box on her dask?
    A. Angry.
    B. Sad.
    C. Disappointed.
    D. Surprised.

32. Which of the following statements is not true?
    A. Tina was not happy on her birthday.
    B. The weather was terrible on that day.
    C. Tina's dog was not feeling well.
    D. Tina's classmates forgot her birthday.

Questions 33~35

Dear Nina,

I'm Derek. Do you remember me? I'm the one you met at Andy's party last Friday. It was nice talking to you.

Let's talk about me first. My favorite sport is basketball. I usually play basketball with my classmates after school. Sometimes I play it with my dad on Sundays. I'm a big fan of NBA, and I love Chauncey Billups best. My dad is an NBA fan too, but he likes Tim Duncan better than Chauncey Billups. We both were crazy about Michael Jordan before, but too bad he doesn't play basketball any more.

As for movies, I prefer action movies, and my favorite movie star is Jacky Chen. Besides, I listen to pop music in my free time. My favorite band is Westlife from England.

That's it for now. How about you? I'm looking forward to hearing from you soon.

Sincerely,
Derek

33. What's Derek's favorite kind of movies?
    A. Love stories.
    B. War movies.
    C. Action movies.
    D. Ghost stories.

34. Who was Derek's favorite basketball player?
    A. Chauncey Billups.
    B. Michael Jordan.
    C. Tim Duncan.
    D. Kevin Garnett.

35. Which of the following statements is not true?
    A. Nina met Derek at a party.
    B. Derek usually plays basketball after school.
    C. Derek's favorite band is Boyzone.
    D. Tim Duncan is Derek's father's favorite NBA star.

2 寫作能力測驗

第一部分　單句寫作

請將答案寫在寫作能力測驗答案紙對應的題號旁，如有拼字、標點、大小寫之錯誤，將予扣分。

第 1～5 題：句子改寫

> 請依題目之提示，將原句改寫成指定型式，並將改寫的句子完整地寫在答案卷上（包括提示之文字及標點符號）。

1. Betty is the smartest girl I've ever seen.
   Betty is _____ than _____.

2. Danny asked me, "Can you get me some stamps?"
   Danny asked me _____.

3. Frank usually goes to school by bus.
   How _____?

4. Why was Eva absent yesterday?
   Do you know _____?

5. Nina cleans the room every morning.
   The room _____.

第 6～10 題：句子合併

> 請依照題目指示，將兩句合併成一句，並將合併的句子完整地寫在答案卷上（包括提示之文字及標點符號）。

6. The man had to take a taxi home.
   His car was towed away.（用 whose）

   _____.

7. John was not at the party last night.
   Jill was not at the party last night.（用 neither... nor...）

   _____.

8. Jane felt sorry.
   She missed her best friend's party.（用 for）

   _____.

9. The baseball game was canceled.
   It rained.（用 because of）

   _____.

10. My mother made me do something.
    I washed the dishes.

   _____.

第 11～15 題：重組

請將題目中所有提示字詞整合成一有意義的句子，並將重組的
句子完整地寫在答案卷上（包括提示之文字及標點符號）。答
案中必須使用所有提示字詞，且不能隨意增加字詞，否則不予
計分。

11. One of _____.
    frightened / loud noise / the girls / by / was / the

12. It is _____.
    smoking / true / is / health / for / that / bad

13. I'll _____.
    rains / stay / if / at home / tomorrow / it

14. You can _____.
    pay / use / either / cash / credit card / or / a

15. I _____.
    with / problem / know / how / deal / don't / to / this

第二部分　段落寫作

請依照題目要求，寫一篇約 50 字的段落。本部分採整體式評分（0～5 級分），再轉換成百分制。評分要點包括重點表達的完整性、文法、用字、拼字、字母大小寫、標點符號。

題目：
Jessie 今天沒有去上學，因為她身體不適。請根據下面的圖片，寫一篇約 **50** 字的短文來敘述她的情況。

第二章　解析卷

1 閱讀能力測驗

本測驗分三部分，全為四選一之選擇題，共 35 題，作答時間
40 分鐘。

第一部分　詞彙和結構

本部分共 15 題，每題含一個空格。請就試題冊上 A、B、C、D 四
個選項中選出最適合題意的字或詞，標示在答案紙上。

Questions 1～15

1. It's pretty _____ to go hiking in such bad weather.
   A. safe
   B. social
   C. talkative
   D. dangerous
   答案：（D）
   中譯：在如此惡劣的天候去健行是很危險的。
   解析：此題考「單字」的用法：
   　　　A. safe　安全的
   　　　B. social　社會的；社交的
   　　　C. talkative　愛說話的，饒舌的
   　　　D. dangerous　危險的
   　　　根據題意，答案應選 D. dangerous（危險的）。

2. This restaurant _____ people. Let's try some others.
   A. is afraid of
   B. is full of
   C. is aware of
   D. is out of

答案：（B）

中譯：這家餐廳客滿，我們到別家去看看。

解析：此題考「片語」的用法：

A. be afraid of 害怕

B. be full of 充滿

C. be aware of 知道

D. be out of 短缺

① Nina is afraid of dogs.

Nina 怕狗。

② The bus is full of people.

這班公車擠滿了人。

③ Are you aware of the danger?

你知道危險嗎？

④ I'm short of money.

我缺錢。

根據上述及題意，答案應選 B. is full of（充滿）。

3. Ben looks smart, but not as _____ as his brother.

A. clever

B. more clever

C. most clever

D. less clever

答案：（A）

中譯：Ben 看起來聰明，但沒有他兄弟那麼聰明。

解析：此題考「原級」用法：

as + Adj + as 與…一樣…

as + Adv + as 與…一樣…

① Lisa is as pretty as Nina.

Lisa 和 Nina 一樣漂亮。

② Mark runs as quickly as John.

Mark 跑步和 John 一樣快。

根據上述，答案應選 A. clever（聰明的）。

其他選項：

B. more clever   後面須接 **than**，表示「比…聰明」

C. most clever   前面須接 **the**，表示「最聰明的」

D. less clever   後面須接 **than**，表示「沒有…來的聰明」

4. Kenny is _____ man I've ever seen.

A. an interesting

B. a more interesting

C. the most interesting

D. a less interesting

答案：（C）

中譯：Kenny 是我見過最有趣的男性。

解析：從 **... I've ever seen**（我所見過的）得知空格須填「最高級形容詞」。所以答案應選 C. the most interesting（最有趣的）。此外，句尾如果是 **... in one's class, ... in one's family**，其前也都用「最高級形容詞」。

5. Let's ask Johnny _____ yesterday.

A. what does the teacher say

B. what did the teacher say

C. what the teacher says

D. what the teacher said

答案：（D）

中譯：我們去問 Johnny 昨天老師說了什麼。

解析：此題考「間接敘述」的用法：

S + V +（O 受詞）+ wh- + S + V

S + V + (O) + wh- + S + Aux（助動詞）+ V原形

① I know what she wants.

我知道她要什麼。

② I asked him when he would go back to Japan.

我問他何時要回日本。

根據上述，答案只能選 D. what the teacher said（老師說了什麼）。

6. Everybody knows _____ Michael Jordan is a famous basketball player.

A. what

B. that

C. how

D. when

答案：（B）

中譯：大家都知道 Michael Jordan 是著名的籃球選手。

解析：此題考「名詞子句」的用法，其句型如下：

S + V + (that) + S + V　（that 可以省略）

S + V + O（受詞）+ (that) + S + V

① I believe that John is an honest student.

我相信 John 是個誠實的學生。

② Eva told me that she didn't do well on the test.

Eva 告訴我說她考試沒有考好。

根據上述，答案應選 B. that。

7. Please _____ your brother while I'm away.

A. take care of

B. take part in

C. get rid of

D. run out of

答案：（A）

中譯：我不在時，請照顧你的弟弟。

解析：此題考「片語」的用法：

A. take care of　照顧

B. take part in　參加（ = participate in = join ）

C. get rid of　去除

D. run out of　用完

根據上述，只有 A. take care of 符合語意。

8. **Derek never misses a single NBA game. He _____ be a basketball fan.**

A. can't

B. couldn't

C. must

D. will

答案：（C）

中譯：Derek 從不錯過美國職業籃球賽，他一定是個籃球迷。

解析：此題考「情態助動詞」的用法：

A. can't　不能；不可能

B. couldn't　不能（用於過去式）

C. must　必須；鐵定

D. will　將

① You can't smoke here.

你不可以在這裡抽煙。

② He has eaten two hamburgers. He can't be hungry now.

他已經吃了兩個漢堡，他現在不可能肚子餓。

③ Sally couldn't go to the party last night because she was sick.

Sally 昨晚無法去參加派對，因為她生病了。

④ You must study hard to please your parents.

你必須用功以取悅你的父母。

⑤ You look like Gina. You must be her sister.

你看起來像 Gina，你一定是她的姊妹。

⑥ We will go mountain climbing on Sunday.

禮拜天我們要去爬山。

根據上述，只有 C. must（鐵定）符合語意。

9. If it rains tomorrow, the game will have to _____.

A. cancel

B. cancels

C. canceling

D. be canceled

答案：（D）

中譯：如果明天下雨，比賽就會取消。

解析：此題考「被動語態」，即 be + p.p.（+ by + 行為者），所以答案應選 D. be canceled（美式拼法），或 be cancelled（英式拼法）。

10. Can anyone help me _____ this bag? It's too heavy for me.

A. carry

B. carrying

C. carried

D. carries

答案：（A）

中譯：有人可以幫我提行李（包包／袋子）嗎？這太重了。

解析：此題考 help 的用法：

help + 人 + V原形

help + 人 + to + V原形

help + 人 + with + 事物

Can you help me (to) do the dishes?

= Can you help me with the dishes?

你可以幫我洗碗嗎？

根據上述，答案應選 A. carry。

11. _____ you home alone when I called you yesterday?

A. Do

B. Did

C. Were

D. Are

答案：（C）

中譯：昨天我打電話給你的時候，你是不是一個人在家？

解析：由... when I **called** you **yesterday**? 得知此題考「過去式」
的用法，所以可消去 A. Do 及 D. Are。另外，從 you
home alone...? 得知空格須填 be 動詞，所以答案只能選
C. Were。

12. Kevin failed the English test. He _____ harder last week.

A. should study

B. should have studied

C. must study

D. must have studied hard

答案：（B）

中譯：Kevin 英文考試不及格，他上週早該用功的。

解析：此題考「情態助動詞」的用法：

should + V原形：表示「義務、建議」，意為「應該」，
用於現在及未來的情況。

should + have + p.p.：表示「義務、建議」，用於過去
的情況。

must + V原形：表示唯一的選擇，或肯定的推論，意
為「必須」、「一定」，用於現在及未來情況。

must + have + p.p.：表示對過去情況的推論，意為
「一定」。

① You should study hard.
　你應該要用功。

② The party **was** great. You **should have come**.
派對很棒，你應該來的。（但卻沒來）

③ You must study hard.
你必須用功。（沒有別的選擇）

④ The ground is wet. It **must have rained** last night.
地面溼答答的，昨晚一定下過雨。

A. should study　應該用功（用於現在及未來的情況）

B. should have studied　早該用功（用於過去的情況）

C. must study　必須用功（用於現在及未來情況）

D. must have studied　那時一定有用功（用於過去情況）

由句子 Kevin **failed** the English test. 得知事件發生在過去，所以空格應填 B. should have studied 或 D. must have studied。但根據語意，則只能選 B. should have studied。

13. An ＿＿＿＿ will be held in the new park tonight.
A. outdoors concert
B. concert outdoors
C. outdoor concert
D. concert outdoor

答案：（C）

中譯：今晚在新公園將舉行露天演唱會／音樂會。

解析：outdoor 為形容詞，意為「戶外的」。
outdoors 為副詞，意為「在戶外」。
所以答案應選 C. outdoor concert（戶外音樂會）。

14. It's not easy for anyone to fall ＿＿＿＿ in Mr. Wang's class. He is so funny.
A. sleep
B. sleeping
C. asleep
D. slept

答案：（C）

中譯：要在王老師的課堂上睡著並不容易，因為他太有趣了。

解析：fall asleep（睡著）。

15. My computer works better and faster than _____.

   A. you

   B. her

   C. its

   D. his

答案：（D）

中譯：我的電腦功能比他的強，速度也比他的快。

解析：此題考「所有格代名詞」的用法：

I → mine

you → yours

he → his

she → hers

we → ours

they → theirs

根據上述，答案應選 D. his。

第二部分 段落填空

本部分共 10 題，包括二個段落，每個段落各含 5 個空格。請就試題冊上 A、B、C、D 四個選項中選出最適合題意的字或詞，標示在答案紙上。

Questions 16～20

Michael and Jenny met at a party one night. For Michael, it was love __(16)__ first sight, but not for Jenny. However, they talked __(17)__ very late at night. When they left the party, it was almost 1 A.M. For the next three months, Michael and Jenny spent every weekend together. They went to the movies, museums, and restaurants together. One night at a nice restaurant, Michael asked Jenny __(18)__ she would marry him, but she said no. The reason was that she was not ready to get married.

Michael was very sad, but he wouldn't __(19)__. He began to write love letters to Jenny every day. In two years, Michael had sent Jenny about 700 love letters. At last, Jenny said, "I'm ready to get married now." To everyone's surprise, the one Jenny wanted to marry was not Michael __(20)__ the mailman who had delivered his love letters to Jenny for two years. She said she began to fall in love with the mail carrier when he delivered Michael's 365th letter to her.

16. A. in
    B. at
    C. for
    D. on

17. A. before
    B. after
    C. once
    D. until

18. A. when
    B. that
    C. unless
    D. if

19. A. stay up
    B. give up
    C. make up
    D. look up

20. A. and
    B. or
    C. but
    D. however

答案：16.（B）　17.（D）　18.（D）　19.（B）　20.（C）

中譯：

> 　　有一天晚上，Michael 和 Jenny 在派對上相遇。對 Michael 而言，那是一見鐘情，但對 Jenny 來說卻不是。然而，那天他們聊得很晚。當他們離開派對時，差不多已是凌晨一點。之後三個月，Michael 和 Jenny 每個週末都在一起。他們一起去看電影、逛博物館和用餐。有一天晚上，在一家美好的餐廳裡，Michael 向 Jenny 求婚，但卻遭到拒絕，原因是女方還沒打算要結婚。
>
> 　　Michael 很傷心，但卻不肯放棄。他開始每天寫情書給Jenny。兩年來，Michael 寫了大約七百封的情書給 Jenny。最後，Jenny 說：「我現在準備要結婚了。」令大家驚訝的是，Jenny 要結婚的對象竟然不是 Michael，而是幫 Michael 送了兩年情書給 Jenny 的那位郵差先生。Jenny 說當郵差送來 Michael 第三百六十五封情書給的她時候，她開始愛上這名郵差。

解析：

16. **at first sight** 第一眼

    They loved each other at first sight.

    他們一見鐘情。

17. A. before 在…之前

    B. after 在…之後

    C. once 一旦；曾經

    D. until 直到（= till）

    根據上述，只有 D. 符合語意，所以答案應選 D. until（直到）。

18. A. when 當

    B. that 引導名詞子句或形容詞子句用

    C. unless 除非

    D. if 是否；假如

    根據上述，只有 D. 符合語意，所以答案應選 D. if（是否）。

19. A. stay up 熬夜

    B. give up 放棄

    C. make up 杜撰；和解；補償（～for）

    D. look up 查閱；向上看；尊敬（～to）

    根據上述，只有 B. 符合語意，所以答案應選 B. give up（放棄）。

20. A. and 和，以及

    B. or 或者

    C. but 而是（not... but...：不是…而是…）；但是

    D. however 然而（須獨立存在）

    Mr. Brown is not John's father but his uncle.

    Brown 先生不是 John 的父親，而是他的叔叔。

    根據上述，只有 C. 符合語意，所以答案只能選 C. but（而是）。

Questions 21~25

Dear Nina,

Long time no see, how's everything? I haven't heard __(21)__ you for a long time. I hope you're doing fine. I have good news __(22)__ you. I have a ten-day vacation from next Friday. Would you like to come and stay with me? There are a lot of things to do and places to go.

I still remember the last time __(23)__ you were here with me. We had great fun. Do you remember the day we went hiking on a cloudy day? We got lost in the mountains and were __(24)__ . My parents called the police for help. When the police found us, we were so cold and hungry __(25)__ we both could hardly move. That was an unforgettable day.

Please let me know if you can come as soon as possible. Say hello to your parents.

Love,
Lisa

21. A. of
    B. from
    C. with
    D. on

22. A. tell
    B. told
    C. telling
    D. to tell

23. A. which
    B. where
    C. when
    D. who

24. A. excited
    B. successful
    C. pleasant
    D. scared

25. **A. that**
   B. as
   C. until
   D. if

答案：21.（B）　22.（D）　23.（C）　24.（D）　25.（A）

中譯：

親愛的 Nina：

　　好久不見，一切可好？已經好久沒有你的消息了，希望你過得好。我有好消息要告訴你，下禮拜五開始我有一連十天的假期，你要不要來我這裡住？我們有好多事情可以做，好多地方可以去。

　　我仍然記得上次你來我這裡，我們玩得好開心。你記得有一次我們陰天去健行的事嗎？我們在山裡迷路了，感到十分害怕。我爸媽報警求助。當警方找到我們的時候，我們又冷又餓，幾乎動不了。那真是難忘的一天。

　　請儘快告訴我你是否可以過來。請向你爸媽問好。

愛你的
Lisa

解析：

21. **hear of**　聽說
    hear from　收到…的信，得到…的消息
    根據上下文，只有 B. 符合語意，所以答案應選 B. from。

22. I have good news to tell you.
    = I have good news for you.
    我有好消息要告訴你。

23. 此題考「關係代名詞」的用法：

    A. which：先行詞為「事、物」。

    B. where：先行詞為「地方」，等於 in which。

    C. when：先行詞為「時間」，等於 that。

    D. who：先行詞為「人」，等於 that。

    從句子 "I still remember the last time _____ you were here with me." 得知關係代名詞的先行詞為 the last time，乃屬於「時間」，所以關係代名詞只能用 C. when。

24. A. excited　感到興奮的

    B. successful　成功的

    C. pleasant　令人愉快的

    D. scared　感到害怕的

    根據上述，只有 D. 符合語意，所以答案應選 D. scared（感到害怕的）。

25. so... that　如此…以至於

    He's so young that he can't go to school.

    = He's too young to go to school.

    他年紀太小不能去上學。

第三部分　閱讀理解

本部分共 10 題，包括數段短文，每段短文後有 1～3 個相關問題，請就試題冊上 A、B、C、D 四個選項中選出最適合者，標示在答案紙上。

Question 26

• **This Platform Is Not In Use** •

26. Where can you see this sign?
   A. In a park.
   B. In a meeting room.
   C. At the train station.
   D. At the airport.

第 26 題

• 本 月 台 暫 不 開 放 •

26. 題目：你在哪裡可以看到這個告示牌？
　　選項：A. 在公園。
　　　　　B. 在會議室。
　　　　　C. 在火車站。
　　　　　D. 在機場。
　　答案：（C）

Questions 27~28

> ### ANDY'S WEAR & BOOTS
> SUMMER SALE
> August 21-31
> 50% off for T-shirts
> 40% off for shirts
> 60% off for shorts
> 30% off for boots
> *HURRY IN BEFORE IT'S TOO LATE*

27. When does Andy's store have a sale?
    A. In June.
    B. In July.
    C. In August.
    D. In September.

28. If a T-shirt costs $300, how much will you have to pay for two T-shirts on sale?
    A. $150.
    B. $200.
    C. $250.
    D. $300.

第 27～28 題

```
    安 迪 服 飾 馬 靴 專 賣 店
         夏 季 特 賣 會
          8月21－31日
          T恤    5折
          襯衫    6折
          短褲    4折
          馬靴    7折
       動 作 要 快
```

27. 題目：安迪的店何時舉辦特賣會？
    選項：A. 在六月。
          B. 在七月。
          C. 在八月。
          D. 在九月。
    答案：（C）

28. 題目：如果一件T恤三百元，那麼兩件打折下來是多少錢？
    選項：A. 一百五十元。
          B. 二百元。
          C. 二百五十元。
          D. 三百元。
    答案：（D）

Questions 29 ~ 30

WONDERLAND CAFE

Lunch Specials

◇ Steak, Potato & Salad   NT$180
◇ Fish, Potato & Salad   NT$150
◇ Chicken, Potato & Salad   NT$120
◇ Pork, Rice & Salad   NT$120

All meals served with bread & your choice of beverage.

29. If you order a chicken special, what will you get besides chicken?
    A. Potato, salad, cake, and tea.
    B. Salad, potato, bread, and coffee.
    C. Potato, salad, and juice.
    D. Salad, rice, and coffee.

30. How much will you have to pay if you and your friends order one steak special and two fish specials?
    A. NT$480.
    B. NT$360.
    C. NT$450.
    D. NT$390.

第 29～30 題

```
                仙  境  餐  館

 商 業 午 餐

 ◇ 牛排、馬鈴薯及沙拉              $180
 ◇ 魚、馬鈴薯及沙拉               $150
 ◇ 雞肉、馬鈴薯及沙拉             $120
 ◇ 豬肉、米飯及沙拉              $120

 所 有 餐 點 均 附 麵 包 及 任 選 的 飲 料
```

29. 題目： 如果你點雞肉特餐，除了雞肉之外，還會附上什麼？

　　選項： A. 馬鈴薯、沙拉、蛋糕及紅茶。

　　　　　B. 沙拉、馬鈴薯、麵包及咖啡。

　　　　　C. 馬鈴薯、沙拉及果汁。

　　　　　D. 沙拉、米飯及咖啡。

　　答案：（B）

30. 題目： 如果你和你的朋友點了一客牛排特餐及兩客魚排特餐，那

　　　　　麼你們要付多少錢？

　　選項： A. 四百八十元。

　　　　　B. 三百六十元。

　　　　　C. 四百五十元。

　　　　　D. 三百九十元。

　　答案：（A）

Questions 31～32

Last Saturday was Tina's birthday, but she was not happy at all. First, the weather was terrible. Then her pet dog was sick. What was worse, many of her friends did not go to her party. She felt very sad, angry and lonely. She cried, "It isn't fair."

However, the next day when she got to the classroom, she found a big box on her desk. She was surprised. It was from her classmates. There were cards, flowers, chocolates and presents in the box. Tina was very excited to see those things. It was a very unforgettable moment for her.

31. How did Tina feel when she found a box on her dask?
    A. Angry.
    B. Sad.
    C. Disappointed.
    D. Surprised.

32. Which of the following statements is not true?
    A. Tina was not happy on her birthday.
    B. The weather was terrible on that day.
    C. Tina's dog was not feeling well.
    D. Tina's classmates forgot her birthday.

第 31～32 題

> 上個禮拜六是 Tina 的生日，但是她一點也不開心。首先，天氣很糟糕。再來，她的愛犬生病了。更慘的是，她很多朋友都沒有去參加她的派對。她非常難過、生氣和寂寞。她大叫：「這不公平！」
>
> 然而，隔天當她到教室的時候，她發現她的桌上有一個大箱子。她很驚訝。那是同學們送的，裡頭有卡片、花、巧克力和禮物。Tina 看到那些東西的時候很興奮。對她來說，那是一個難忘的時刻。

31. 題目：當 Tina 發現她的桌上有一個箱子時，她的心情如何？
    選項：A. 生氣。
    　　　B. 難過。
    　　　C. 失望。
    　　　D. 驚訝。
    答案：（D）

32. 題目：以下何者為非？
    選項：A. Tina 生日當天並不開心。
    　　　B. 當天天氣十分惡劣。
    　　　C. Tina 的狗生病了。
    　　　D. Tina 的同學們忘了她的生日。
    答案：（D）

Questions 33～35

> Dear Nina,
>
> I'm Derek. Do you remember me? I'm the one you met at Andy's party last Friday. It was nice talking to you.
>
> Let's talk about me first. My favorite sport is basketball. I usually play basketball with my classmates after school. Sometimes I play it with my dad on Sundays. I'm a big fan of NBA, and I love Chauncey Billups best. My dad is an NBA fan too, but he likes Tim Duncan better than Chauncey Billups. We both were crazy about Michael Jordan before, but too bad he doesn't play basketball any more.
>
> As for movies, I prefer action movies, and my favorite movie star is Jacky Chen. Besides, I listen to pop music in my free time. My favorite band is Westlife from England.
>
> That's it for now. How about you? I'm looking forward to hearing from you sôon.
>
> *Sincerely,*
> *Derek*

33. What's Derek's favorite kind of movies?
   A. Love stories.
   B. War movies.
   C. Action movies.
   D. Ghost stories.

34. Who was Derek's favorite basketball player?
   A. Chauncey Billups.
   B. Michael Jordan.
   C. Tim Duncan.
   D. Kevin Garnett.

35. Which of the following statements is not true?

A. Nina met Derek at a party.

B. Derek usually plays basketball after school.

C. Derek's favorite band is Boyzone.

D. Tim Duncan is Derek's father's favorite NBA star.

第 33～35 題

親愛的 Nina：

　　我是 Derek，妳還記得我嗎？我就是上星期五在 Andy 的派對上與妳相識的那個人。能跟妳聊天很愉快。

　　首先自我介紹一下：我最喜歡的運動是籃球，通常在放學後跟同學打籃球，有時候會在禮拜天跟我爸一起打球。我很迷美國職籃，最喜歡的是 Chauncey Billups。我爸也是個美國職籃迷，不過他喜歡 Tim Duncan 甚於 Chauncey Billups。我們以前都很迷 Michael Jordan，只可惜他已經不再打籃球了。

　　至於電影，我比較喜歡動作片，最喜愛的電影明星是成龍。此外，空閒時我聽流行音樂，最喜歡的樂團是來自英國的西城男孩。

　　就這樣，妳呢？盼望很快能聽到妳的消息。

誠摯的

Derek

33. 題目：Derek 最喜歡的電影類型為何？

　　選項：A. 文藝愛情片。

　　　　　B. 戰爭片。

　　　　　C. 動作片。

　　　　　D. 鬼片。

　答案：（C）

解析： cartoon　卡通影片；動畫（= animation）

　　　 horror film/movie　恐怖片

　　　 science fiction movie　科幻片

　　　 thriller　驚悚片

　　　 drama　劇情片

　　　 documentary　紀錄片

　　　 comedy　喜劇

　　　 tragedy　悲劇

　　　 farce　鬧劇

34. 題目： 誰曾是 Derek 最喜愛的籃球員？

　　 選項： A. Chauncey Billups。

　　　　　 B. Michael Jordan。

　　　　　 C. Tim Duncan。

　　　　　 D. Kevin Garnett。

　　 答案：（B）

35. 題目： 下列何者為非？

　　 選項： A. Nina 與 Derek 在派對上相遇。

　　　　　 B. Derek 通常放學後打籃球。

　　　　　 C. Derek 最喜歡的樂團是男孩特區（Boyzone）。

　　　　　 D. Tim Duncan 是 Derek 父親最喜愛的美國職籃明星。

　　 答案：（C）

2 寫作能力測驗

請將答案寫在寫作能力測驗答案紙對應的題號旁，如有拼字、標點、大小寫之錯誤，將予扣分。

第 1～5 題：句子改寫

> 請依題目之提示，將原句改寫成指定型式，並將改寫的句子完整地寫在答案卷上（包括提示之文字及標點符號）。

1. Betty is the smartest girl I've ever seen.

Betty is _____ than _____.

答案：Betty is **smarter** than **any other girl I've ever seen.**

　　　= Betty is **smarter** than **all the other girls I've ever seen.**

中譯：Betty 是我見過最聰明的女孩。

解析：此題考形容詞最高級與比較級的代換用法，其句型如下：

(1) S + be + the + Adj-est + N

　　= S + be + Adj-er + than + any other + N

　　= S + be + Adj-er + than + all the other + N-s

(2) S + be + the + most + Adj（三音節(含)以上）+ N

　　= S + be + more + Adj（三音節(含)以上）+ than + any other + N

　　= S + be + more + Adj（三音節(含)以上）+ than + all the other + N-s

① Ben is the tallest boy in his class.

　= Ben is taller than any other boy in his class.

　= Ben is taller than all the other boys in his class.

Ben 是他班上最高的男孩。

② Sandy is the most beautiful girl (that) I've ever seen.

= Sandy is more beautiful than any other girl (that) I've ever seen.

= Sandy is more beautiful than all the other girls (that) I've ever seen.

Sandy 是我見過最美麗的女孩。

2. Danny asked me, "Can you get me some stamps?"
Danny asked me _____.

答案： Danny asked me **if I could get him some stamps.**

= Danny asked me **whether I could get him some stamps (or not).**

= Danny asked me **whether or not I could get him some stamps.**

中譯： Danny 問我是否可以幫他買幾張郵票。

解析： 此題考直接敘述與間接敘述互換的用法，其句型如下：

S + asked + O, "Aux + S + V原形?"

= **S + asked + O + if/whether + S + Aux過去式 + V原形**

S + asked + O, "Wh-word + Aux + S + V原形?"

= **S + asked + O + wh-word + S + V過去式**

① She asked me, "Can you help me?"

= She asked me **if I could** help **her.**

= She asked me **whether I could** help **her.**

她問我是否願意幫助她。

② Mark asked me, "Where does Tina live?"

= Mark asked me **where Tina lived.**

Mark 問我 Tina 住在哪裡。

※ 注意間接敘述的時態及人稱變化。

間接敘述的相關例句請參考姊妹作《全民英檢初級保證班》「文法要點 **12**」名詞子句。

3. Frank usually goes to school by bus.

How _____?

答案：How **does Frank usually go to school**?

中譯：Frank 通常搭何種交通工具上學？

解析：從句尾 **by bus** 得知此題考交通工具，其句型如下：

How + do/does/did + S + V

① "How does your father usually go to work?"

"By bus."

「你爸爸是怎麼去上班的？」

「搭公車。」

② "How did you get here?"

"On foot."

「你怎麼到這裡來的？」

「走路來的。」

③ "How do you go to school?"

"I usually go to school by car." or "I usually drive to school."

「你是怎麼去上學的？」

「我通常開車去上學。」

4. Why was Eva absent yesterday?

Do you know _____?

答案：Do you know **why Eva was absent yesterday**?

中譯：你知道為什麼 Eva 昨天缺席嗎？

解析：此題考名詞子句的用法，其句型如下：

Do you know + wh-word + S (+ Aux) + V...?

Do you know + if/whether + S (+ Aux) + V...?

① Do you know why **Lisa was** so angry?

= Do you know the reason why Lisa was so angry?

你知道 Lisa 為何如此生氣嗎？

② Do you know when **he will** come?

你知道他何時會來嗎？

③ Do you know if **she will** come?

= Do you know whether (or not) **she will** come?

= Do you know whether **she will** come or not?

你知道她是否會來？

5. Nina cleans the room every morning.

The room _____.

答案：The room is cleaned by Nina every morning.

中譯：這房間每天早上都由 Nina 負責打掃。

解析：此題考被動形式的用法，其句型如下：

S + be + p.p. + by + O

① Derek washes the dishes every evening.

= The dishes **are wished by** Derek every evening.

Derek 每天晚上洗碗。

② Sally mopped the floor this morning.

= The floor **was mopped by** Sally this morning.

這地板是 Sally 早上拖的。

※ 被動式的用法及相關例句，請參考姊妹作《全民英檢初級
保證班》「文法要點 8」被動語態。

第 6～10 題：句子合併

請依照題目指示，將兩句合併成一句，並將合併的句子完整地
寫在答案卷上（包括提示之文字及標點符號）。

6. The man had to take a taxi home.

His car was towed away.（用 whose）

_____.

答案：The man whose car was towed away had to take a taxi home.

中譯：車子被拖吊的那個男的必須搭計程車回家。

解析：此題考形容詞子句的用法。由於關係代名詞為所有格，所以須用 **whose**。

S + whose + N + V... + V

S + V + O + whose + N + V...

① The woman whose son was missing cried very hard.

兒子失蹤的那個婦人哭得很傷心。

② Yesterday I met John, whose father was my high school teacher.

昨天我碰到 John，他爸爸是我的高中老師。

※ 例句 ① 為形容詞子句之限定用法（無逗點），而例句 ② 為非限定用法（有逗點），其區別與用法請參考姊妹作《全民英檢初級保證班》「文法要點 12」形容詞子句。

7. John was not at the party last night.

Jill was not at the party last night.（用 neither... nor...）

_____.

答案：Neither John nor Jill was at the party last night.

中譯：John 和 Jill 昨晚都不在派對上。

解析：此題考 **neither... nor...** 的用法，其句型如下：

Neither + S1 + nor + S2 + V

S + neither + V + nor + V

S + V + neither + A + nor + B

① Neither Jim nor his younger sister is hard-working.

Jim 和他的妹妹都不是很勤奮。

② He neither smokes nor drinks.
他不抽煙也不喝酒。

③ Betty speaks neither English nor Chinese.
Betty 既不說英語也不說中文。

※ **neither... nor...**：不是…也不是…。動詞形式須視 **nor** 後面的「名詞」而定。

8. Jane felt sorry.
She missed her best friend's party.（用 **for**）

_____.

答案：Jane felt sorry for missing her best friend's party.

中譯：Jane 因為錯過她至友的派對而感到抱歉／遺憾。

解析：此題考 **sorry** 的用法，其句型如下：

S + feel/be + sorry + for + V-ing

① My dad felt sorry for yelling at you.
我爸因為對你怒吼而感到抱歉。

② I'm sorry for calling so late.
很抱歉這麼晚還打電話過去。

※ **I'm sorry <u>about</u> that.**

feel 的動詞三態變化：**feel, felt, felt**

9. The baseball game was canceled.
It rained.（用 **because of**）

_____.

答案：The baseball game was canceled because of the rain.

中譯：棒球賽因雨取消。

解析：此題考 **because of** 的用法，其句型如下：

S + V + because of + N

= S + V + because + S + V

① We canceled the picnic because of the heavy rain.
= We canceled the picnic because it rained heavily.
我們因為下大雨而取消了野餐活動。

② Tammy didn't go to school because of her sickness/ illness.

= Tammy didn't go to school because she was sick/ ill.

Tammy 沒有去上學，因為她生病了。

10. My mother made me do something.
I washed the dishes.

_____.

答案：My mom made me wash the dishes.

中譯：我媽要我洗碗。

解析：此題考使役動詞（如 make, have）的用法，其句型如下：

S + make/have + O + V原形　逼使…；叫…

① My father made me eat breakfast before going to school.

我父親叫我吃完早餐才能去上學。

② I'll have John fix your computer.

我會叫 John 修理你的電腦。

受詞若為事物，則後接過去分詞，表示「請別人處理」。

I'll have your computer **fixed**.

= I'll have someone **fix** your computer.

我會請人修理你的電腦。我會拿你的電腦去送修。

※ I'll <u>get</u> John <u>to fix</u> your computer.

我會叫 John 修理你的電腦。

I'll get it <u>done</u> by Tuesday.

禮拜二以前我會把它弄好。

Please <u>let</u> him <u>go</u>.

請讓他去。請放他走。

The music makes me (feel) happy.

這音樂使我（感到）快樂。

第 **11**～**15** 題：重組

> 請將題目中所有提示字詞整合成一有意義的句子，並將重組的
> 句子完整地寫在答案卷上（包括提示之文字及標點符號）。答
> 案中必須使用所有提示字詞，且不能隨意增加字詞，否則不予
> 計分。

11. One of _____.
frightened / loud noise / the girls / by / was / the

答案：One of **the girls was frightened** by the loud noise.

中譯：其中一個女孩被這個巨響嚇到。

解析：此題考被動式的用法，其句型如下：

S + be + p.p. + by + O

① One of the boys **was hit** by a car.
其中有一個男孩被車撞了。

② Two of the girls **were scolded** by the teacher.
其中兩個女孩被老師責備。

12. It is _____.
smoking / true / is / health / for / that / bad

答案：It is **true that smoking is bad for health.**

中譯：抽煙有害健康是千真萬確的事。

解析：此題考名詞子句與虛主詞的用法，其句型如下：

It is + Adj/N + that + S + V

① It is true that Nina is a pretty girl.
沒錯，Nina是個漂亮的女孩。

② It is a fact that drunken driving is dangerous.
酒醉駕駛很危險，這是一項事實。

上述例句亦可將名詞子句移至句首當主詞：

① **That** Nina is a pretty girl is true.

② **That** drunken driving is dangerous is a fact.

13. I'll _____.

rains / stay / if / at home / tomorrow / it

答案：I'll **stay at home if it rains** tomorrow.

中譯：如果明天下雨，我就待在家裡。

解析：此題考假設語氣的用法，其句型如下：

(1) 能發生的假設法：

If + S + V, S + will/can + V原形

(2) 與現在事實相反的假設法：

If + S + V過去式**, S + would/could + V**原形

(3) 與過去事實相反的假設法：

If + S + had + p.p., S + would/could + have + p.p.

① If it is fine tomorrow, I **will go** hiking.

= I **will go** hiking if it is fine tomorrow.

如果明天好天氣的話，那我會去健行。

（至於明天天氣是好是壞，無從得知）

② If I **had** enough money, I **would buy** a motorbike.

= I **would buy** a motorbike if I **had** enough money.

如果我現在有足夠的錢，那我會去買機車。

③ If I **had had** enough money, I **would have gone** abroad.

= I **would have gone** abroad if I **had had** enough money.

如果那時候我有足夠的錢，那我早就出國了。

（就是因為當時沒有足夠的錢，所以沒有出國。）

※ **If** 的其他句型及例句，請參考姊妹作《全民英檢初級保證班》「文法要點 **11**」假設語氣。

14. You can _____.

pay / use / either / cash / credit card / or / a

答案：You can **either pay cash or use a credit card**.

中譯：你可以付現或刷卡。

解析：此題考 **either... or...** 的用法，其句型如下：

S + Aux + either + V原形 **+ or + V**原形

S + V + either + A + or + B

Either + S1 + or + S2 + V

① You may/can either take a test or write a term paper.

你可以參加考試或者寫期末報告。

※ **term**：學期。

② Jimmy loves either Helen or Sandy.

Jimmy 愛的不是 Helen 就是 Sandy。

③ Either Tom or John did this.

這件事不是 Tom 做的就是 John 做的。

15. I _____.

with / problem / know / how / deal / don't / to / this

答案：I don't know how to deal with this problem.

中譯：我不知道如何處理這個問題。

解析：此題考名詞子句的用法，其句型如下：

S + V + how to + V + O

S + V + what to + V

S + V + wh-word + S + V

① I know how to solve the problem.

我知道怎麼解決這個問題。

② I don't know what to do.

= I don't know what I should do.

我不知道該怎麼辦。

③ I know where Michael lives.

我知道 Michael 住哪裡。

※ 名詞子句的其他相關用法及例句請參考姊妹作《全民英檢初級保證班》「文法要點 **12**」子句。

第二部分　段落寫作

請依照題目要求，寫一篇約 50 字的段落。本部分採整體式評分
（0～5 級分），再轉換成百分制。評分要點包括重點表達的完整
性、文法、用字、拼字、字母大小寫、標點符號。

題目：

Jessie 今天沒有去上學，因為她身體不適。請根據下面的圖
片，寫一篇約 **50** 字的短文來敘述她的情況。

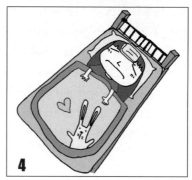

參考範文：

Jessie went to the night market with her family yesterday. She ate a lot of foods there such as stinky tofu, noodles, fried chicken, etc. She also had lots of ice and drinks. Although Jessie had a good time at the night market, she did not feel very well when she got home. She did not go to school today because she had to stay in bed.

中譯：

Jessie 昨天跟她家人去逛夜市。她在那裡吃了很多食物，像是臭豆腐、麵條、炸雞等等。同時她也吃了很多冰及飲料。雖然 Jessie 在夜市玩得很開心，但是當她回到家時，覺得不太舒服。她今天沒有去上學，因為她必須躺在床上休息。

解析：

(1) 第一句 "Jessie went to the night market with her family yesterday." 點出主題：Jessie 昨天從事的活動。
(2) 接著依據主題發展內容，說明她活動的細節。
(3) 最後以吃壞肚子而無法去上學作結。
(4) 時態用過去式，符合描述文的時態要求。
(5) 善用簡單句 "Jessie went to the night market with her family yesterday." "She also had lots of ice and drinks." 及複句 "Although Jessie had a good time at the night market, she did not feel very well when she got home." "She did not go to school today because she had to stay in bed."。
(6) 文章前後呼應，一氣呵成。

重要單字片語：

night market　夜市

a lot of = lots of = many = much　很多

such as = like = for example = for instance　例如，像是

stinky tofu　臭豆腐

noodles　麵

fried chicken　炸雞

also　也

drinks　飲料（soft drinks = soda 汽水）

have a good time = have fun　玩得開心

get home　到家

had to　必須（只用於過去）

stay in bed　躺在床上，臥病在床

第四組

Part IV

Practice Test 4

第一章 試題卷

1 閱讀能力測驗

本測驗分三部分，全為四選一之選擇題，共 35 題，作答時間 40 分鐘。

第一部分　詞彙和結構

本部分共 15 題，每題含一個空格。請就試題冊上 A、B、C、D 四個選項中選出最適合題意的字或詞，標示在答案紙上。

Questions 1～15

1. Kevin practices _____ English every day.
   A. speak
   B. to speak
   C. speaking
   D. spoke

2. John, you look _____ fatter than you were last year.
   A. many
   B. much
   C. a few
   D. little

3. Lucy can speak _____.
   A. English good
   B. a good English
   C. English well
   D. a well English

4. I saw several homeless people on my way _____.
   A. to home
   B. come home
   C. at home
   D. home

5. _____ students passed the English conversation test.
   A. Most of
   B. The most
   C. The most of
   D. Most of the

6. John is really good _____ playing computer games.
   A. on
   B. at
   C. with
   D. for

7. Ben usually spends two hours _____ English every day.
   A. study
   B. to study
   C. studied
   D. studying

8. Collecting coins _____ my favorite hobby.
   A. are
   B. is
   C. has
   D. have

9. "Sorry, I forgot _____ you a present," said the husband.
   A. to buy
   B. buying
   C. buy
   D. bought

10. Kelly asked Johnny, "When will you _____ home tonight?"
    A. get to
    B. take
    C. arrive at
    D. get

11. Do remember to _____ the medicine after meals three times a day.
    A. make
    B. get
    C. take
    D. eat

12. I _____ a trip to Kenting last summer.
    A. took
    B. got
    C. make
    D. do

13. Jessica's only fifteen years old, so she's _____ to get married.
    A. young enough
    B. enough young
    C. not young
    D. too young

14. I _____ live in the country in Nanto.

    A. use to

    B. used to

    C. am used to

    D. used

15. You look great _____ that T-shirt.

    A. on

    B. for

    C. in

    D. at

第二部分 　段落填空

本部分共 10 題，包括二個段落，每個段落各含 5 個空格。請就試題冊上 A、B、C、D 四個選項中選出最適合題意的字或詞，標示在答案紙上。

Questions 16～20

Dear Ann:

　　It's hard for me to write to you because I haven't written letters for a long time.

　　I've been living in this country for five years, and I've been taking care of children at home ＿（16）＿ I got here. I'm a patient woman ＿（17）＿ loves working with children. ＿（18）＿ fact, I'd like to have a full-time job outside the home at a day-care center. I'm writing ＿（19）＿ I'm having an interview next Wednesday. I'm nervous and worried. Are there any ＿（20）＿ for me?

Best wishes,
Judy from L.A.

---

16. A. for
　　B. since
　　C. as
　　D. when

17. A. which
　　B. where
　　C. whom
　　D. who

18. A. In
    B. For
    C. On
    D. At

19. A. although
    B. if
    C. because
    D. when

20. A. interests
    B. hobbies
    C. decisions
    D. tips

Questions 21～25

It's __(21)__ the law for parents to leave small children alone in public or at home in the United States. __(22)__ do most working people do? Sometimes grandparents or other family members look after small children. Sometimes parents hire a babysitter to take care of their small children. Sometimes parents __(23)__ their small children at a day-care center. Some school children go to a relative's house or a neighbor's home after school. __(24)__ children go to clubs or other fun places __(25)__ adults can watch them. Parents pick up their children after work.

21. A. for
    B. against
    C. in
    D. with

22. A. Where
    B. Who
    C. When
    D. What

23. A. leave
    B. left
    C. take
    D. took

24. A. Another
    B. Other
    C. The other
    D. The others

25. A. who
    B. which
    C. where
    D. when

本部分共 10 題，包括數段短文，每段短文後有 1～3 個相關問題，請就試題冊上 A、B、C、D 四個選項中選出最適合者，標示在答案紙上。

Question 26

• NO PHOTOGRAPHY •

26. What is the purpose of this sign?
   A. To tell you how to take photos.
   B. To warn you not to take pictures.
   C. To show you where to buy a camera.
   D. To stop you from entering the room.

Questions 27～28

DEREK'S BURGERS

Burgers		Side Orders		Drinks	
Hamburger	$30	French Fries	$25	Soda	$20
Cheeseburger	$35	Onion Rings	$30	Coffee	$30
Chickenburger	$45	Salad	$35	Tea	$25
Fishburger	$45	Corn Soup	$20	Milkshake	$35
Double Cheeseburger	$50				
Double Hamburger	$45				

27. What's not available at Derek's Burgers?
    A. Milkshakes.
    B. Fishburgers.
    C. Onion rings.
    D. Ice cream.

28. How much would you have to pay if you ordered two cheeseburgers, two onion rings and two coffees?
    A. $180.
    B. $190.
    C. $200.
    D. $210.

Questions 29～30

DEREK'S——*for less expensive, easier shopping*

Take a look at Derek's leather skirt — only $150,
which sells for $1,000 in Paris.
Also, add only $20 for a cool sweater.
Why go to Paris when you can get top fashion at Derek's?

29. How much cheaper is the same leather skirt sold at Derek's than in Paris?
    A. $750.
    B. $830.
    C. $850.
    D. $930.

30. How much would you have to pay if you bought two leather skirts and a sweater at Derek's?
  A. $320.
  B. $300.
  C. $2000.
  D. $2200.

Questions 31~32

Dear Sally,

　　It's great to write you this letter.

　　First of all, let me introduce myself. I was born in Taipei, the biggest city in Taiwan. My father teaches math in high school, and my mother runs a small bookstore. I have one older sister and one younger brother. My older sister, Jessica, studies English in college. She always helps me with my schoolwork, especially in English. My younger brother, Robby, is in the second grade. He's very clever and cute.

　　As for me, I'm thirteen years old and will graduate from junior high school next year. In my free time, I like to play basketball, go hiking and listen to music. How about you?

Best wishes,
Andy

31. What's not Andy's hobby?
  A. Playing basketball.
  B. Listening to music.
  C. Hiking.
  D. Swimming.

32. **How many people are there in Andy's family?**
    A. Four.
    B. Five.
    C. Six.
    D. Seven.

Questions 33~35

> What kind of food do you like?
> Do you eat raw fish? Dog meat? Stinky tofu? People usually like to eat food that they know well and dislike food that look, smell or taste strange. For example, the Japanese like eating raw fish (sashimi), but few Americans would ever taste it. Many Chinese people love eating dog meat, which is surprising to westerners. Some people do not eat certain food for religious reasons. For example, people in India do not eat beef because they consider cattle holy animals.
> What about you? Do you have special eating habits?

33. **Who loves to eat raw fish?**
    A. Americans.
    B. Australians.
    C. The Chinese.
    D. The Japanese.

34. Which of the following statements is not true?
    A. Many Chinese love dog meat.
    B. Many westerners enjoy raw fish.
    C. People in India do not eat beef.
    D. Cows are considered holy animals in India.

35. What's a good title for the reading?
    A. Fast Food.
    B. Raw Fish and Dog Meat.
    C. Eating Habits.
    D. People Cannot Live Without Food.

2 寫作能力測驗

第一部分   單句寫作

請將答案寫在寫作能力測驗答案紙對應的題號旁,如有拼字、標點、大小寫之錯誤,將予扣分。

第 **1~5** 題:句子改寫

> 請依題目之提示,將原句改寫成指定型式,並將改寫的句子完整地寫在答案卷上(包括提示之文字及標點符號)。

1. There are five people in John's family.
   How many _____?

2. Can you lend me two hundred dollars?
   May I _____?

3. The news surprised me.
   I _____.

4. Playing computer games is fun.
   It _____.

5. Ben spent two thousand dollars on that jacket.
   That jacket _____.

第 6～10 題：句子合併

> 請依照題目指示，將兩句合併成一句，並將合併的句子完整地
> 寫在答案卷上（包括提示之文字及標點符號）。

6. Where does Jim live?
   I don't know.
   I _____.

7. He is rich.
   He is not very happy.（用 although）
   _____.

8. My mom will be back.
   She will be back at 10:30.（用 not... until）
   _____.

9. The city was beautiful.
   We spent our summer vacation in this city.
   （用關係代名詞 where）
   _____.

10. The job is too difficult.
    I can't do the job.（用 so... that）
    _____.

第 11~15 題：重組

> 請將題目中所有提示字詞整合成一有意義的句子，並將重組的
> 句子完整地寫在答案卷上（包括提示之文字及標點符號）。答
> 案中必須使用所有提示字詞，且不能隨意增加字詞，否則不予
> 計分。

11. She _____.
    me / whether / I / problem / asked / me / could / the /
    solve

12. I _____.
    swim / to / really / to / want / how / learn

13. Neither _____!
    solve / of / could / that / them / problem

14. I _____.
    call / get / you / will / as / soon / I / there / as

15. It _____.
    thirty / get / about / to / minutes / takes / there

第二部分 段落寫作

請依照題目要求,寫一篇約 50 字的段落。本部分採整體式評分
(0~5 級分),再轉換成百分制。評分要點包括重點表達的完整
性、文法、用字、拼字、字母大小寫、標點符號。

題目:
Linda 想要減肥,請根據圖片寫一篇約 **50** 字的短文,來說
明她減肥的經過。

第二章　解析卷

1 閱讀能力測驗

本測驗分三部分，全為四選一之選擇題，共 35 題，作答時間 40 分鐘。

第一部分　詞彙和結構

本部分共 15 題，每題含一個空格。請就試題冊上 A、B、C、D 四個選項中選出最適合題意的字或詞，標示在答案紙上。

Questions 1～15

1. Kevin practices _____ English every day.
A. speak
B. to speak
C. speaking
D. spoke
答案：（C）
中譯：Kevin 每天練習說英語。
解析：practice + V-ing　練習…

2. John, you look _____ fatter than you were last year.
A. many
B. much
C. a few
D. little
答案：（B）
中譯：John 你看起來比去年胖很多。
解析：比較級 fatter 前只可接 much, a lot 或 far。

3. Lucy can speak _____.

A. English good

B. a good English

C. English well

D. a well English

答案：（C）

中譯：Lucy 英語說得好。

解析：to speak English well = to speak good English

4. I saw several homeless people on my way _____.

A. to home

B. come home

C. at home

D. home

答案：（D）

中譯：在回家路上，我看見幾個遊民。

解析：on my way home　在回家路上，home 在此當「副詞」用

on my way to school　在上學途中

on my way to **the** station　在往車站的途中

5. _____ students passed the English conversation test.

A. Most of

B. The most

C. The most of

D. Most of the

答案：（D）

中譯：大部分學生都通過英語會話考試。

解析：此題考 **most** 的用法：

most + 複數名詞 = most of the + 複數名詞＝the majority

of + 複數名詞　大多數的…

6. John is really good _____ playing computer games.
   A. on
   B. at
   C. with
   D. for
   答案：（B）
   中譯：John 真的很會玩電腦遊戲。
   解析：be good at　擅長於

7. Ben usually spends two hours _____ English every day.
   A. study
   B. to study
   C. studied
   D. studying
   答案：（D）
   中譯：Ben 通常每天花兩個小時讀英文。
   解析：**spend + 時間 + V-ing**　花時間從事⋯
          spend + 時間 + on + N　花時間在⋯上面

8. Collecting coins _____ my favorite hobby.
   A. are
   B. is
   C. has
   D. have
   答案：（B）
   中譯：收集銅板是我最喜歡的嗜好。
   解析：此題考「主詞與 be 動詞一致」的觀念，由 **Collecting coins**（收集銅板）可知其後 be 動詞須用「單數」的 **is**，因指「收集銅板這項嗜好」，而非指銅板的數量。而 C. has 則與題意不符。

9. "Sorry, I forgot _____ you a present," said the husband.
A. to buy
B. buying
C. buy
D. bought

答案：（A）

中譯：「對不起，我忘了買禮物給你。」丈夫說道。

解析：**forget to + V**　表示「忘了去做」某事
　　　forget + V-ing　表示「忘了有做過」某事
　　　根據題意，此題應選 A. to buy。

10. Kelly asked Johnny, "When will you _____ home tonight?"
A. get to
B. take
C. arrive at
D. get

答案：（D）

中譯：Kelly 問 Johnny：「你今晚幾點會到家？」

解析：**get home**　到家（＝ arrive home）
　　　get to Taipei　抵達台北（＝ arrive in Taipei）
　　　get to the airport　到達機場（＝ arrive at the airport）

11. Do remember to _____ the medicine after meals three times a day.
A. make
B. get
C. take
D. eat

答案：（C）

中譯：務必記得飯後吃藥，一天三次。

解析：此題考慣用語 take the medicine（吃藥）。

12. I _____ a trip to Kenting last summer.

A. took

B. got

C. make

D. do

答案：（A）

中譯：去年夏天我去墾丁旅行。

解析：此題考片語 took a trip to（到…旅行），為「過去」事件。

13. Jessica's only fifteen years old, so she's _____ to get married.

A. young enough

B. enough young

C. not young

D. too young

答案：（D）

中譯：Jessica 才十五歲，所以她年紀太小而不能結婚。

解析：此題考句型 too... to（太…而不能）的用法。而 A. young enough（夠年輕）與題意不符；B. enough young 文法有誤；D. not young 與題意不符。

14. I _____ live in the country in Nanto.

A. use to

B. used to

C. am used to

D. used

答案：（B）

中譯：我以前住在南投的鄉下。

解析：**used to + V**原形　表示過去的習慣或事實

be used to + Ving/N　表示現在已習慣於某種行為、事物或狀態

① I used to get up early.

我以前常早起。

② I'm used to getting up early.

我現在習慣早起。

③ You'll get/be used to it soon.

你很快就會習慣的。

由於空格後為「動詞原形」**live**，所以答案只能選 B. used to。

15. You look great _____ that T-shirt.

A. on

B. for

C. in

D. at

答案：（C）

中譯：你穿那件 T 恤很好看。

解析：You look great **in** that T-shirt.

= That T-shirt looks great **on** you.

第二部分　段落填空

本部分共 10 題，包括二個段落，每個段落各含 5 個空格。請就試題冊上 A、B、C、D 四個選項中選出最適合題意的字或詞，標示在答案紙上。

Questions 16～20

Dear Ann:

　　It's hard for me to write to you because I haven't written letters for a long time.

　　I've been living in this country for five years, and I've been taking care of children at home （16） I got here. I'm a patient woman （17） loves working with children. （18） fact, I'd like to have a full-time job outside the home at a day-care center. I'm writing （19） I'm having an interview next Wednesday. I'm nervous and worried. Are there any （20） for me?

Best wishes,
Judy from L.A.

---

16. A. for
　　B. since
　　C. as
　　D. when

17. A. which
　　B. where
　　C. whom
　　D. who

18. A. In
    B. For
    C. On
    D. At

19. A. although
    B. if
    C. because
    D. when

20. A. interests
    B. hobbies
    C. decisions
    D. tips

答案：16.（B）　17.（D）　18.（A）　19.（C）　20.（D）

中譯：

親愛的 Ann：

　　要我寫信給你並不容易，因為我已經好久沒有提筆寫信了。

　　我住在這個國家已有五年，而自從我到這裡以來，就一直在家裡照顧小孩。我是個很有耐心的女性，喜歡跟小孩相處。事實上，我想在托兒所有份全職的工作。我現在寫信是因為下星期三我要參加一個面試，我感到既緊張又擔心。有沒有什麼應試的訣竅呢？

給你最佳的祝福
來自洛杉磯的 Judy

解析：

16. 由... I've been taking care of children in my home ＿＿＿＿＿ I got here, 可知此題考 **since** 的用法，其句型為：**S + have/has + been + Ving + since + S + V過去式**，所以答案應選 B. since。

17. 此題考「關係代名詞」的用法，因為空格前（先行詞）為人（**a patient woman**），所以答案只能選 who。

18. 此題考片語 **in fact**（事實上）。

19. 由 "I'm writing ＿＿＿＿ I'm having an interview next Wednesday." 得知，空格前後文表示「因果」關係，所以答案應選 C. because。

20. 此題考「用字」：
    A. interests　興趣
    B. hobbies　嗜好
    C. decision　決定
    D. tips　訣竅
    根據上述，只有 D. 符合語意，所以答案應選 D. tips（訣竅）。

Questions 21～25

It's **（21）** the law for parents to leave small children alone in public or at home in the United States. **（22）** do most working people do? Sometimes grandparents or other family members look after small children. Sometimes parents hire a babysitter to take care of their small children. Sometimes parents **（23）** their small children at a day-care center. Some school children go to a relative's house or a neighbor's home after school. **（24）** children go to clubs or other fun places **（25）** adults can watch them. Parents pick up their children after work.

21. A. for
    B. against
    C. in
    D. with

22. A. Where
    B. Who
    C. When
    D. What

23. A. leave
    B. left
    C. take
    D. took

24. A. Another
    B. Other
    C. The other
    D. The others

25. A. who
    B. which
    C. where
    D. when

答案：21.（B）　22.（D）　23.（A）　24.（B）　25.（C）

中譯：

在美國，把幼兒獨自留在公共場所或家裡是違法的。那麼大部分的上班族怎麼辦？有時候由祖父母或其他家人照顧幼兒；有時候父母雇用褓姆來照顧幼兒；有時候父母會把幼兒交給托兒所。有些孩童放學後會去親戚家或鄰居家。有些孩童則到一些有大人照顧的社團或遊樂場，父母下班後就去接他們。

解析：

21. 此題考 It's **against** the law for 人 to V（做…是違法的行為）。

22. 既然不能把幼兒獨自留置在任何地方，則上班族怎麼辦？由上下文得知空格須填 D. What，以符合題意。

23. 此題考「用字」及「時態」：
   leave... in　把…留置於
   take... to　帶…去
   由於前後文談的都是「目前的情況」，所以只能用「現在簡單式」。
   take 後面不接 in，因此只有 A. leave 符合題意與時態。

24. 此題考「對應用字」。由於前句 **Some...**，所以空格須填 Other 以為對應。其意為：有些…而有些（其他）…。

25. 此題考「關係代名詞」的用法：
   A. who　先行詞為「人」
   B. which　先行詞為「事物」
   C. where　先行詞為「地方」（= in which）
   D. when　先行詞為「時間」
   由於空格前之先行詞為 other fun **places**，所以答案只能選 C. where。

第三部分 閱讀理解

本部分共 10 題，包括數段短文，每段短文後有 1～3 個相關問題，請就試題冊上 A、B、C、D 四個選項中選出最適合者，標示在答案紙上。

Question 26

NO PHOTOGRAPHY

26. What is the purpose of this sign?
    A. To tell you how to take photos.
    B. To warn you not to take pictures.
    C. To show you where to buy a camera.
    D. To stop you from entering the room.

第 26 題

不　　准　　攝　　影

26. 題目：這個告示牌的目的為何？
    選項：A. 告訴你攝影的技巧。
    　　　B. 警告你不准攝影。
    　　　C. 指示你購買相機的地方。
    　　　D. 禁止你進入房間。
    答案：（B）

Questions 27~28

DEREK'S BURGERS

Burgers		Side Orders		Drinks	
Hamburger	$30	French Fries	$25	Soda	$20
Cheeseburger	$35	Onion Rings	$30	Coffee	$30
Chickenburger	$45	Salad	$35	Tea	$25
Fishburger	$45	Corn Soup	$20	Milkshake	$35
Double Cheeseburger	$50				
Double Hamburger	$45				

27. What's not available at Derek's Burgers?

    A. Milkshakes.

    B. Fishburgers.

    C. Onion rings.

    D. Ice cream.

28. How much would you have to pay if you ordered two cheeseburgers, two onion rings and two coffees?

    A. $180.

    B. $190.

    C. $200.

    D. $210.

第 27～28 題

Derek 漢堡店				
漢 堡		**附 餐**		**飲 料**
漢　堡	$30	薯　條	$25	汽水　$20
吉士堡	$35	洋蔥圈	$30	咖啡　$30
雞肉堡	$45	沙　拉	$35	紅茶　$25
魚　堡	$45	玉米濃湯	$20	奶昔　$35
雙層吉士堡	$50			
雙層漢堡	$45			

27. 題目：Derek 漢堡店不賣什麼東西？

　　選項：A. 奶昔。

　　　　　B. 魚堡。

　　　　　C. 洋蔥圈。

　　　　　D. 冰淇淋。

　　答案：（D）

28. 題目：如果你點兩份吉士堡、兩份洋蔥圈及兩杯咖啡，那你要付
　　　　　多少錢？

　　選項：A. 一百八十元。

　　　　　B. 一百九十元。

　　　　　C. 二百元。

　　　　　D. 二百一十元。

　　答案：（B）

Questions 29~30

> ### DEREK'S——*for less expensive, easier shopping*
>
> *Take a look at Derek's leather skirt—only $150,*
> *which sells for $1,000 in Paris.*
> *Also, add only $20 for a cool sweater.*
> *Why go to Paris when you can get top fashion at Derek's?*

29. **How much cheaper is the same leather skirt sold at Derek's than in Paris?**
    A. $750.
    B. $830.
    C. $850.
    D. $930.

30. **How much would you have to pay if you bought two leather skirts and a sweater at Derek's?**
    A. $320.
    B. $300.
    C. $2000.
    D. $2200.

第 **29～30** 題

DEREK's —— *購物更便宜，更容易*

來看看 Derek's 的皮裙——只要一百五十元，
這在巴黎要賣一千元。
同時，只要再加二十元，就可以獲得酷帥毛衣。
在 Derek's 就可買到頂級時裝，何苦要遠赴巴黎？

---

29. 題目：同樣的裙子在 Derek's 的售價比在巴黎便宜多少？
    選項：A. 七百五十元。
    　　　B. 八百三十元。
    　　　C. 八百五十元。
    　　　D. 九百三十元。
    答案：（C）

30. 題目：如果你在 Derek's 買兩件皮裙和一件毛衣，那你要付多少錢？
    選項：A. 三百二十元。
    　　　B. 三百元。
    　　　C. 二千元。
    　　　D. 二千二百元。
    答案：（A）

Questions 31～32

> Dear Sally,
>
> It's great to write you this letter.
>
> First of all, let me introduce myself. I was born in Taipei, the biggest city in Taiwan. My father teaches math in high school, and my mother runs a small bookstore. I have one older sister and one younger brother. My older sister, Jessica, studies English in college. She always helps me with my schoolwork, especially in English. My younger brother, Robby, is in the second grade. He's very clever and cute.
>
> As for me, I'm thirteen years old and will graduate from junior high school next year. In my free time, I like to play basketball, go hiking and listen to music. How about you?
>
> *Best wishes,*
>
> *Andy*

31. What's not Andy's hobby?
   A. Playing basketball.
   B. Listening to music.
   C. Hiking.
   D. Swimming.

32. How many people are there in Andy's family?
   A. Four.
   B. Five.
   C. Six.
   D. Seven.

第 31～32 題

親愛的 Sally,

很高興能寫這封信給你。

首先,我來自我介紹。我出生於台北——台灣最大的城市。我父親在中學教數學,而我母親在經營一家小書店。我有一個姊姊和一個弟弟。我姊姊 Jessica 在大學唸英文系。她總是協助我的功課,尤其是英文方面。我弟弟 Robby 現在是小二,他既聰明又可愛。

至於我,我今年十三歲,明年即將從國中畢業。有空的時候,我喜歡打籃球、健行和聽音樂。妳呢?

祝福你

Andy

---

31. 題目:下列何者並非 Andy 的嗜好?

選項:A. 打籃球。

B. 聽音樂。

C. 健行。

D. 游泳。

答案:(D)

32. 題目:Andy 家中有多少人口?

選項:A. 四人。

B. 五人。

C. 六人。

D. 七人。

答案:(B)

Questions 33~35

> What kind of food do you like?
>
> Do you eat raw fish? Dog meat? Stinky tofu? People usually like to eat food that they know well and dislike food that look, smell or taste strange. For example, the Japanese like eating raw fish (sashimi), but few Americans would ever taste it. Many Chinese people love eating dog meat, which is surprising to westerners. Some people do not eat certain food for religious reasons. For example, people in India do not eat beef because they consider cattle holy animals.
>
> What about you? Do you have special eating habits?

33. Who loves to eat raw fish?
    A. Americans.
    B. Australians.
    C. The Chinese.
    D. The Japanese.

34. Which of the following statements is not true?
    A. Many Chinese love dog meat.
    B. Many westerners enjoy raw fish.
    C. People in India do not eat beef.
    D. Cows are considered holy animals in India.

35. What's a good title for the reading?
    A. Fast Food.
    B. Raw Fish and Dog Meat.
    C. Eating Habits.
    D. People Cannot Live Without Food.

第 33～35 題

你喜歡吃什麼樣的食物？

你吃生魚（片）嗎？狗肉呢？臭豆腐呢？人們通常都吃他們所熟悉的食物，而不喜歡吃那些看起來、聞起來或嚐起來奇怪的食物。例如，日本人喜歡吃生魚（片），但很少有美國人願意去嚐嚐看。很多中國人喜歡吃狗肉，這對西方人來說是很不可思議的。也有些人為了宗教理由而不吃某些食物。例如，印度人不吃牛肉，因為他們認為牛是神聖的動物。

你呢？你有特殊的飲食習慣嗎？

33. 題目：誰喜歡吃生魚（片）？
    選項：A. 美國人。
          B. 澳洲人。
          C. 中國人。
          D. 日本人。
    答案：（D）

34. 題目： 下列敘述何者為非？
   　選項： A. 很多中國人喜歡吃狗肉。

   　　　　 B. 很多西方人喜歡吃生魚（片）。

   　　　　 C. 印度人不吃牛肉。

   　　　　 D. 牛在印度被認為是神聖的動物。

   　答案：（B）

35. 題目： 下列何者可做為此篇文章的標題？
   　選項： A. 速食。

   　　　　 B. 生魚（片）與狗肉。

   　　　　 C. 飲食習慣。

   　　　　 D. 人們必須依賴食物而生存。

   　答案：（C）

2 寫作能力測驗

第一部分　單句寫作

請將答案寫在寫作能力測驗答案紙對應的題號旁，如有拼字、標點、大小寫之錯誤，將予扣分。

第 1～5 題：句子改寫

> 請依題目之提示，將原句改寫成指定型式，並將改寫的句子完整地寫在答案卷上（包括提示之文字及標點符號）。

1. There are five people in John's family.

  How many _____?

  答案：How many **people are there in John's family**?

  中譯：John 的家庭成員有幾人？

  解析：此題考 **How many** 的用法，其句型如下：

  How many + N + are + there...?

  ① How many students are there in this class?
     這個班有幾個學生？

  ② "How many cars are there?"
     "There are four." or "There's only one."
     「有幾部車？」
     「有四部。」或「只有一部。」

2. Can you lend me two hundred dollars?

  May I _____?

  答案：May **I borrow two hundred dollars from you**?

  中譯：我可以跟你借兩百元嗎？

解析：此題考 borrow 和 lend 及疑問句的用法，其句型如下：

Can + you + lend + me/her/him... + 物?（借出）

= Can + you + lend + 物 + to + me/her/him...?

= May/Can + I/she/he... + borrow + 物 + from + you?（借入）

① Can you lend me your car?

    = Can you lend your car to me?

    = Can/May I borrow your car?

    你能把車借給我嗎？

② Can you lend John one million dollars?

    = Can John borrow one million dollars from you.

    = Can you lend one million dollars to John?

    你能借 John 一百萬元嗎？

3. The news surprised me.

I _____.

答案：I was surprised at the news.

中譯：我對這個消息感到驚訝。

解析：此題考情緒動詞（surprise）的用法，其句型如下：

S + be + surprised + at + O

S + surprise + O

We were surprised at the news.

= The news surprised us.

= The news was surprising to us.

我們對這個消息感到驚訝。這消息使我們感到驚訝。

(1) 情緒動詞雖為被動的形態（be+p.p.）但卻具有主動的意義，因此其後的介系詞通常不是 by，而是 at, with, in 等。

(2) 其他情緒動詞的用法，尚有 be excited **about**, be satisfied **with**, be pleased **with**, be bored **with**, be disappointed **at** 等。

    ① They were excited about the basketball game.

        = The basketball game was exciting to them.

        = The basketball game excited them.

        他們看籃球賽看得很過癮。

② I'm interested in pop music.

   = Pop music is interesting to me.

   = Pop music interests me.

   我對流行音樂有興趣。

③ I was bored with the show.

   = The show was boring to me.

   = The show bored me.

   我對這個表演／節目感到無聊。

④ The boss was not satisfied with my report.

   = My report was not satisfying/satisfactory to the boss.

   = My report did not satisfy the boss.

   老闆不滿意我的報告。

⑤ They're pleased with our service.

   = Our service is pleasing/pleasant to them.

   = Our service pleases them.

   他們很滿意我們的服務。

⑥ We were disappointed at what he did.

   = What he did was disappointing to us.

   = What he did disappointed us.

   我們對他的所作所為感到失望。

4. Playing computer games is fun.

   It _____.

   答案：It is fun to play computer games.

   　　　= It is fun playing computer games.

   中譯：玩電腦遊戲很有趣。

   解析：此題考動名詞、不定詞與虛主詞的代換用法，其句型如下：

   It is Adj/N + to + V原形

   It is Adj/N + V-ing

   V-ing + is + Adj/N

   To + V + is + Adj/N

① It is bad to hurt animals.
傷害動物是不好的。

② It is a nice surprise to see you here.
在這裡遇到你真是令人驚喜。

③ It is dangerous to stay out too late.
在外面待太晚很危險。

④ It is a great joy staying with my grandmother.
跟奶奶住是很快樂的。

⑤ Smoking is bad.
= To smoke is bad.
抽煙不好。

⑥ To eat vegetables is a must.
= Eating vegetables is a must.
吃蔬菜是必要的。

※ 動名詞與不定詞的相關用法及例句，請參考姊妹作《全民英檢初級保證班》「文法要點 6」動名詞、「文法要點 7」不定詞以及「寫作題型全都錄」。

5. Ben spent two thousand dollars on that jacket.
That jacket _____.

答案： That jacket **cost Ben two thousand dollars**.

中譯： 那件夾克花了 Ben 兩千元。

解析： 此題考 spend 與 cost 的代換用法，其句型如下：

人 + **spend** + 錢 + **on** + 物品

物品 + **cost** + 人 + 錢

I spent $500 on the shoes.

= The shoes cost me $500.

這雙鞋花了我五百元。

(1) spend 的三態變化為：**spend, spent, spent**
cost 的三態變化為：**cost, cost, cost**

(2) How much does it cost?
= How much is it?
這要多少錢？

(3) I **paid** $100 **for** the swimsuit.

= I spent $100 on the swimsuit.

= The swimsuit cost me $100.

這套泳衣花了我一百元。

第 6~10 題：句子合併

請依照題目指示，將兩句合併成一句，並將合併的句子完整地寫在答案卷上（包括提示之文字及標點符號）。

6. Where does Jim live?
I don't know.

I _____.

答案：I don't know where Jim lives.

中譯：我不知道 Jim 住在哪裡。

解析：此題考名詞子句的用法，其句型如下：

S + V + wh-word + S + V

S + V + if/whether + S + V

S + V + that + S + V

① I know why Jenny left her country.

= I know the reason why Jenny left her country.

我知道 Jenny 為什麼會離開她的國家。

② I don't know if Kenny will come tomorrow.

= I don't know whether Kenny will come tomorrow or not.

= I don't know whether (or not) Kenny will come tomorrow.

我不知道 Kenny 明天會不會來。

③ I believe (that) May is an honest girl.
我相信 May 是個誠實的女孩。

7. He is rich.
He is not very happy.（用 although）

_____.

答案： Although he is rich, he is not very happy.
= He is not very happy although he is rich.

中譯： 雖然他有錢，但卻不快樂。

解析： 此題考附屬連接詞 **although**（雖然）的用法，其句型如下：

Although + S + V, S + V

S + V + although + S + V

Although he is poor, he is happy.

= He is happy although he is poor.

= He is poor, but/yet he is happy.

他人雖窮，但卻很快樂。

(1) although = though

(2) although（雖然）與 but（但是）不可同時出現，即「漢賊不兩立」也。

(3) 上句亦可寫成：

He is happy in spite of his poverty.

= In spite of his poverty, he is happy.

8. My mom will be back.
She will be back at 10:30.（用 not... until）

_____.

答案： My mom will not be back until 10:30.

中譯： 我媽十點半才會回來。

解析： 此題考 **not ... until** 的用法，其句型如下：

S + will not + V原形 + until + 時間（表未來）

S + will not + V原形 + until + S + V現在式（表未來）

S + did not + V原形 + until + 時間（表過去）

S + did not + V原形 + until + S + V過去式（表過去）

① The boss will **not** be back **until** Friday.

老闆禮拜五才會回來。

② She will not come home until her mother agrees.

她要她媽媽同意才會回家。

③ I did not go to bed until 2:00 a.m.

我到清晨兩點才去睡覺。

④ I did not do my homework until my dad came home.

我一直到我爸回家才去寫功課。

※ **I'll wait here until she comes back.**

我要在這裡等到她回來。

9. **The city was beautiful.**

We spent our summer vacation in this city.

（用關係代名詞 where）

_____.

答案：The city where we spent our summer vacation was beautiful.

中譯：我們去渡假的那座城市很美。

解析：此題考形容詞子句的限定用法，由於先行詞是地方（the city），所以關係代名詞須用 where，其句型如下：

S + where + S + V + V

The office building **where Ella works** is beautiful.

= The office building **in which Ella works** is beautiful.

Ella 上班的那棟辦公大樓很漂亮。

若先行詞十分明確，則其後須加「逗點」，而成非限定用法：

① I don't like Taipei, where the traffic is terrible.

我不喜歡台北，因為那裡的交通很糟糕。

② Derek, whose mother is a Taiwanese teacher, can speak Taiwanese.

媽媽是台語老師的 Derek 會講台語。

（也許因為媽媽是台語老師，所以 Derek 會講台語。）

10. The job is too difficult.
I can't do the job.（用 so... that）

_____.

答案： The job is so difficult that I can't do it.

中譯： 這工作太難了，我沒辦法做。

解析： 此題考 so... that（如此…以致於）的用法，其句型如下：

S + be + so + Adj + that + S + V

① It was so hot that I took off my coat.

天氣太熱了，所以我脫掉外套。

② John was so fat that he couldn't get into the taxi.

John 太胖了，以致於無法坐進計程車裡。

※ **He walked so quickly that I couldn't catch up with him.**

他走太快了，我趕不上他。

第 **11**～**15** 題：重組

請將題目中所有提示字詞整合成一有意義的句子，並將重組的句子完整地寫在答案卷上（包括提示之文字及標點符號）。答案中必須使用所有提示字詞，且不能隨意增加字詞，否則不予計分。

11. She _____.

whether / I / problem / asked / me / could / the / solve

答案：She **asked me whether I could solve the problem**.

中譯：她問我是否能解決這個問題。

解析：此題考含 **whether** 的名詞子句之用法，其句型如下：

S + V (+ O) + whether + S + V

① I don't know whether Michael will help us.

我不知道 Michael 是否會幫助我們。

① Tina asked me whether I would study abroad.

Tina 問我是否要出國唸書。

※ **Whether Peter will come or not is not important.**

Peter 要不要來並不重要。

Whether you like it or not, you'll have to take the test.

不管你喜歡與否，你都必須參加這次考試。

12. I _____.

swim / to / really / to / want / how / learn

答案：I really want to learn how to swim.

中譯：我真的很想學游泳。

解析：此題考 **want to** 及 **learn** 的用法，其句型如下：

S + (really) want to + learn + how to + V原形

① I want to learn how to cook.

我想學做菜。

② She really wants to learn how to be popular.

她真的很想學習如何受人歡迎。

13. Neither _____!

solve / of / could / that / them / problem

答案：Neither of them could solve that problem!

中譯：他們兩個人都無法解決那個問題。

解析：此題考 **neither**（兩者皆不）的用法，其句型如下：

Neither of them + V單數

Neither + N + V單數

① Neither of them is honest.
他們兩個都不誠實。

② Neither story is true.
兩則故事都不是真的。

※ **Both of his sisters are not married.**
他的兩個姊妹並非都已結婚。（即一個結婚，一個未婚。）
Neither of his sisters is married.
他的兩個姊妹都未婚。

14. I _____.

call / get / you / will / as / soon / I / there / as

答案：I will call you as soon as I get there.

中譯：我一到那裡，就打電話給你。

解析：此題考 **as soon as**（一…就）的用法，其句型如下：
S + will + V + as soon as + S + V
I'll give you a call as soon as I get to Australia.
我一到澳洲，就電話給你。

※ **as soon as** 亦可用於過去情況：
It began to rain as soon as I got home.
我一到家，就開始下雨了。

15. It _____.

thirty / get / about / to / minutes / takes / there

答案：It takes about thirty minutes to get there.

中譯：到那裡差不多要三十分鐘。

解析：此題考 **take**（花費）的用法，其句型如下：
It + takes (+ O) + 時間 + to + V原形（表現在）
It + took (+ O) + 時間 + to + V原形（表過去）
It + will take (+ O) + 時間 + V原形（表未來）

① It takes about two hours to get to the airport from here.
從這裡到機場大約要兩小時。

② It took me a long time to finish the report.

我花了好長的時間才完成報告。

③ It will take a lot of time to make them say yes.

要他們同意將要花很長的時間。

※ **It takes courage to say no to them.**

= To say no to them takes courage.

= Saying no to them takes courage.

拒絕他們需要勇氣。

It takes a lot of effort to learn a language well.

= To learn a language well takes a lot of effort.

= Learning a language well takes a lot of effort.

學好語言需要花很多的功夫。

第二部分　段落寫作

請依照題目要求，寫一篇約 50 字的段落。本部分採整體式評分（0～5 級分），再轉換成百分制。評分要點包括重點表達的完整性、文法、用字、拼字、字母大小寫、標點符號。

題目：
Linda 想要減肥，請根據圖片寫一篇約 50 字的短文，來說明她減肥的經過。

參考範文：

　　Linda was on a diet because she was heavy and wanted to look better. First, she said no to all kinds of fast food. Then she went jogging every day after school. It was not an easy job for her at first, but she didn't give up. Finally, she became thinner and looked better.

中譯：

　　Linda 因為過胖而想要讓自己好看一點，所以她就去減肥。首先，她拒絕所有的速食。其次，她每天放學後去慢跑。對她來說，一開始那不是一件容易的事，但是她沒有放棄。最後，她終於變瘦了，而且也變好看了。

解析：

(1) 第一句 "Linda was on a diet because she was heavy and wanted to look better." 點出本文主題：Linda 身材不佳而想藉由減肥來增加自己的魅力。

(2) 接著根據主題句說明她減肥的過程。

(3) 善用轉折詞（First, Then），使短文更顯流暢。

(4) 時態用過去式，符合描述文的時態要求。

(5) 善用各類句型，如簡單句 "First, she said no to all kinds of fast food."、複合句（"It was not an easy job for her at first, but she didn't give up." 以及複句 "Linda was on a diet because she was heavy...". 當然五大基本句型皆散見於各類變化句型當中。

(6) 文章前後呼應，一氣呵成。

第一組

閱讀能力測驗

1.（B）　2.（C）　3.（D）　4.（C）　5.（A）　6.（B）
7.（A）　8.（C）　9.（B）　10.（D）　11.（B）　12.（B）
13.（C）　14.（B）　15.（A）　16.（A）　17.（D）　18.（A）
19.（C）　20.（D）　21.（A）　22.（D）　23.（A）　24.（B）
25.（C）　26.（C）　27.（A）　28.（C）　29.（D）　30.（C）
31.（D）　32.（C）　33.（B）　34.（C）　35.（C）

寫作能力測驗

1. Did Miss Lin teach her students nicely?
2. How often does John go to the movies?
3. Please tell me where Jenny is.
4. It takes a lot of work to pass the test.
5. That pen is cheaper than this one.
   = That pen is less expensive than this one.
   = That pen is not so/as expensive as this one.
6. Do you hear John singing in the bathroom?
7. Do you know the woman (who is) talking on the phone?
8. Mike hurt his foot while he was playing basketball.
   = While Mike was playing basketball, he hurt his foot.
9. Both Lisa and Eva live in Taipei.
10. Mark has been playing computer games since 9:00.
11. They left in a hurry yesterday.
12. Landy has been playing the piano for ten years.
13. An active reader usually concentrates on one thing at a time.
14. She is the most popular English teacher at school.
15. What a smart boy he is!

段落寫作參考範文：

On my way home yesterday, I saw a fast motorcycle following a taxi very closely. Suddenly, the taxi stopped, and the motorcycle hit the taxi. The motorcyclist fell to the ground and was badly hurt. He cried out in pain. Soon the police officers came to deal with the accident, and the motorcyclist was sent to the hospital in an ambulance.

第二組

閱讀能力測驗

1.（C）	2.（D）	3.（B）	4.（A）	5.（C）	6.（A）
7.（B）	8.（D）	9.（D）	10.（A）	11.（A）	12.（B）
13.（C）	14.（A）	15.（B）	16.（C）	17.（B）	18.（C）
19.（D）	20.（C）	21.（C）	22.（D）	23.（A）	24.（C）
25.（B）	26.（D）	27.（B）	28.（C）	29.（C）	30.（D）
31.（D）	32.（B）	33.（D）	34.（D）	35.（B）	

寫作能力測驗

1. How long have they lived in Taipei?
2. They are factory workers.
3. Tim went swimming yesterday.
4. It is dangerous to ride a motorcycle with one hand.
5. She told me not to listen to Michael.
6. We stayed at a hotel which was near a lake.
7. Penny loves swimming, and so does her sister.
8. Not only my father but also my mother is a teacher.

9. Jenny left the office without telling anyone.

10. Bill went swimming instead of studying for the test.

   = Instead of studying for the test, Bill went swimming.

11. There were a few car accidents yesterday.

12. Across from my house is a city library.

13. The cake that your mom made tasted great.

14. Michael enjoys playing computer games with his friends after school.

15. I lost my wallet while I was jogging in the park.

段落寫作參考範文：

It is a Sunday morning, and there are a lot of people in the park. Some are taking a walk, some are chatting, some are playing ball, some are walking their dogs, some are dancing, and some are reading. It is a sunny day, and it is good for people to spend a Sunday morning in a park.

第三組

閱讀能力測驗

1.（D）	2.（B）	3.（A）	4.（C）	5.（D）	6.（B）
7.（A）	8.（C）	9.（D）	10.（A）	11.（C）	12.（B）
13.（C）	14.（C）	15.（D）	16.（B）	17.（D）	18.（D）
19.（B）	20.（C）	21.（B）	22.（D）	23.（C）	24.（D）
25.（A）	26.（C）	27.（C）	28.（D）	29.（B）	30.（A）
31.（D）	32.（D）	33.（C）	34.（B）	35.（C）	

寫作能力測驗

1. Betty is smarter than any other girl I've ever seen.

   = Betty is smarter than all the other girls I've ever seen.

2. Danny asked me if I could get him some stamps.

   = Danny asked me whether I could get him some stamps (or not).

   = Danny asked me whether or not I could get him some stamps.

3. How does Frank usually go to school?

4. Do you know why Eva was absent yesterday?

5. The room is cleaned by Nina every morning.

6. The man whose car was towed away had to take a taxi home.

7. Neither John nor Jill was at the party last night.

8. Jane felt sorry for missing her best friend's party.

9. The baseball game was canceled because of the rain.

10. My mom made me wash the dishes.

11. One of the girls was frightened by the loud noise.

12. It is true that smoking is bad for health.

13. I'll stay at home if it rains tomorrow.

14. You can either pay cash or use a credit card.

15. I don't know how to deal with this problem.

段落寫作參考範文：

Jessie went to the night market with her family yesterday. She ate a lot of foods there such as stinky tofu, noodles, fried chicken, etc. She also had lots of ice and drinks. Although Jessie had a good time at the night market, she did not feel very well when she got home. She did not go to school today because she had to stay in bed.

閱讀能力測驗

1. (C)	2. (B)	3. (C)	4. (D)	5. (D)	6. (B)
7. (D)	8. (B)	9. (A)	10. (D)	11. (C)	12. (A)
13. (D)	14. (B)	15. (C)	16. (B)	17. (D)	18. (A)
19. (C)	20. (D)	21. (B)	22. (D)	23. (A)	24. (B)
25. (C)	26. (B)	27. (D)	28. (B)	29. (C)	30. (A)
31. (D)	32. (B)	33. (D)	34. (B)	35. (C)	

寫作能力測驗

1. How many people are there in John's family?

2. May I borrow two hundred dollars from you?

3. I was surprised at the news.

4. It is fun to play computer games.

    = It is fun playing computer games.

5. That jacket cost Ben two thousand dollars.

6. I don't know where Jim lives.

7. Although he is rich, he is not very happy.

    = He is not very happy although he is rich.

8. My mom will not be back until 10:30.

9. The city where we spent our summer vacation was beautiful.

10. The job is so difficult that I can't do it.

11. She asked me whether I could solve the problem.

12. I really want to learn how to swim.

13. Neither of them could solve that problem!

14. I will call you as soon as I get there.

15. It takes about thirty minutes to get there.

段落寫作參考範文：

Linda was on a diet because she was heavy and wanted to look better. First, she said no to all kinds of fast food. Then she went jogging every day after school. It was not an easy job for her at first, but she didn't give up. Finally, she became thinner and looked better.

A

above   *adj.* 以上的   *prep.* 在…之上

absent ←→ present   *adj.* 缺席的 ←→ 出席的

accident   *n.* 意外事故

accidentally = by chance = by accident   *adv.* 偶然地，不經意地

across   *adv. prep.* 橫越；在…的對面

action   *n.* 行動；動作（take action 採取行動）

activity   *n.* 活動   *adj.* active 積極的；活潑的

actually   *adv.* 實際上

add   *v.* 加上（～to）

address   *n.* 住址；演講（= speech）

adult = grownup   *n.* 成人   *adj.* 成人的

advertisement = ad   *n.* 廣告

advice   *n.* 建議，勸告（永遠單數形）   *v.* advise

airplane = plane   *n.* 飛機

airport   *n.* 機場

allow   *v.* 允許（～to + V）

almost = nearly   *adv.* 幾乎

alone   *adj. adv.* 單獨的（地）（= by oneself）；只有

America   *n.* 美國

American   *n.* 美國人   *adj.* 美國的

angry   *adj.* 生氣的   *n.* anger

animal   *n.* 動物

anybody = anyone   *n.* 任何人

apartment   *n.* 公寓

apologize   *v.* 道歉   *n.* apology

April   *n.* 四月

asleep   *adv. adj.* 睡著（的）（fall asleep）

attend   *v.* 出席   *n.* attendance

attention   *n.* 注意（pay attention to）   *adj.* attentive

ATTN   致，收件者（= attention）

attract   *v.* 吸引   *n.* attraction 吸引力   *adj.* atractive 迷人的

August   *n.* 八月

Australian   *n.* 澳洲人   *adj.* 澳洲（人）的

available   *adj.* 可以獲得的；有空的

avoid   *v.* 避免（～V-ing）

B

badly   *adv.* 很壞地；非常地

bag   *n.* 袋子，包包

band   *n.* 樂隊，樂團

bank   *n.* 銀行（bank teller 銀行員）

basketball   *n.* 籃球

bathroom   *n.* 浴室

beach   *n.* 海邊，沙灘

beautiful   *adj.* 美麗的   *n.* beauty

beef   *n.* 牛肉

before   *prep.* 在…之前   *conj.* 在…之前   *adv.* 以前

begin   *v.* 開始   *n.* beginning

believe   *v.* 相信，認為

beside = next to   *prep.* 在…的旁邊

besides   *adv.* 此外（= in addition）
   prep. 除了…之外（包括）（= in addition to)

bill   *n.* 帳單；法案

billion   *n.* 十億

birthday   *n.* 生日

boots   *n.* 靴子

bored   *adj.* 感到無聊的

boring   *adj.* 無聊的

Boston   *n.* 波士頓

both   *adj. pron.* 兩者（的）

bowl   *n.* 碗；保齡球   *v.* 打保齡球

bread   *n.* 麵包

broken   *adj.* 故障的；斷裂的

brown   *adj. n.* 棕色（的）

busy   *adj.* 忙碌的（～V-ing）

C

cafe   *n.* 小餐廳；咖啡館

cake   *n.* 蛋糕

camera   *n.* 照相機

can   *n.* 罐子

Canada   *n.* 加拿大

cancel = call off   *v.* 取消

card   *n.* 卡片；名片；紙牌

carefully ⟷ carelessly   *adv.* 小心地，仔細地 ⟷ 不小心地

careless ⟷ careful   *adj.* 不小心的，馬虎的，不仔細的 ⟷ 小心的

carry   *v.* 攜帶，拿

cash   *n.* 現金

cause   *v.* 造成；導致（= result in = lead to）   *n.* 原因（= reason）

cell phone = mobile phone   *n.* 手機（為 cellular phone 的簡稱）

center   *n.* 中心

certain   *adj.* 某種；確定的

change   *v.* 改變   *n.* 變化；零錢

cheat   *v.* 作弊；欺騙

cheeseburger   *n.* 吉士堡

Chicago   *n.* 芝加哥

chicken   *n.* 雞；雞肉

chickenburger   *n.* 雞肉堡

chips   *n.* 洋芋片

chocolate   *n.* 巧克力

choose = pick out   *v.* 選擇（過去式為 chose）

city   *n.* 城市

class   *n.* 課程；班級

classmate   *n.* 同學

classroom   *n.* 教室

clean　　*v.* 清理　*adj.* 乾淨的

clerk　　*n.* 職員

clever　　*adj.* 聰明的

climb　　*v.* 爬（山、樹…）

close　　*adj.* 親近的；密切的；靠近的（～to）　*v.* 關上

closely　　*adv.* 密切地；靠近地；仔細地

cloudy　　*adj.* 陰天的　*n.* cloud 雲；陰影

club　　*n.* 社團；俱樂部

coin　　*n.* 銅板，硬幣

coke　　*n.* 可樂

cold　　*n.* 感冒（have a cold = catch (a) cold）　*adj.* 寒冷的

collect　　*v.* 收集

comfortable ⟷ uncomfortable
　adj. 舒適的；自在的 ⟷ 不舒服的；不自在的

company　　*n.* 公司

computer　　*n.* 電腦

concert　　*n.* 音樂會，演唱會

confident　　*adj.* 有信心的（～of）　*n.* confidence

consider = think over　　*v.* 認為；考慮

contact　　*v. n.* 連絡

continue　　*v.* 繼續（～V-ing 或 ～to + V = go on + V-ing）

convenient
　adj. 方便的　*n.* convenience（convenience store 便利商店）

conversation　　*n.* 會話

cook　　*v.* 做飯　*n.* 廚師（cooker 廚具）

cookies　　*n.*（甜）餅乾、西點（複數形）

cool　　*adj.* 酷的；棒的；涼爽的

cost　　*v.* 花費；值　*n.* 費用；價格

country　　*n.* 國家；鄉下（in the country ⟷ in the city）

crackers　　*n.*（鹹）餅乾

crazy　　*adj.* 瘋狂的；著迷的（～about）

cross　　*v.* 橫越（= go across）　*n.* 十字架

cry　　*v. n.* 哭泣；大叫

curious　　*adj.* 好奇的（～about）

customer   *n.* 顧客

D

dad = daddy   *n.* 爸爸

dangerous   *adj.* 危險的   *n.* danger（in danger 有危險）

date   *n.* 約會；棗子   *v.* 與…約會

December   *n.* 十二月

decide   *v.* 決定（～to + V = make up one's mind to + V）

decision   *n.* 決定，決策

deep   *adj.* 深的

definition   *n.* 定義

delicious = tasty   *adj.* 美味的

deliver   *v.* 遞送，投遞   *n.* delivery

destination   *n.* 目的地

diary   *n.* 日記（keep a diary 寫日記）

die   *v.* 死亡   *adj.* dead   *n.* death

diet   *n.* 醫生規定的飲食；節食（go/be on a diet）

diet coke   *n.* 健怡（飲料名）

different   *adj.* 不同的

difficult ⟷ easy/simple   *adj.* 困難的 ⟷ 容易的

disagree ⟷ agree   *v.* 不同意 ⟷ 同意

disappointed   *adj.* 感到失望的（～at）   *n.* disappointment 失望

disappointing   *adj.* 令人失望的（～to）

discuss = talk over   *v.* 討論

disease   *n.* 疾病

dislike   *v. n.* 不喜歡

display   *v. n.* 展示；表現；炫耀（= show off）

Doraemon   *n.* 哆啦A夢（卡通人物的名稱）

dress   *n.* 洋裝，衣服   *v.* 穿衣

drinks   *n.* 飲料（複數形）（soft drinks = soda 汽水）

E

early ⟷ late   *adj. adv.* 早的（地）⟷ 晚的（地）

earthquake = quake   *n.* 地震

easy ⟷ difficult = hard   *adj.* 容易的 ⟷ 困難的

elect   *v.* 選舉 *n.* election

embarrassed   *adj.* 感到困窘的 *n.* embarrassment

embarrassing   *adj.* 令人感到困窘的，很糗的 *v.* embarrass 使困窘

engineer   *n.* 工程師

England   *n.* 英格蘭；英國

enjoy   *n.* 享受，享有（～V-ing）

enjoyable   *adj.* 令人愉快的

enter   *v.* 進入；登記參加 *n.* entrance 入口

especially = above all   *adv.* 尤其

event   *n.* 事件；活動

everybody = everyone   *n.* 每人

everywhere = here and there   *adv.* 到處

exam = examination = test   *n.* 考試

except ⟷ besides
  prep. 除了…之外（不包括）⟷ 除了…之外（包括）

excite   *v.* 使興奮 *adj.* excited 感到興奮的（～about）

exciting   *adj.* 刺激的，過癮的

exercise   *v. n.* 運動（= get/do exercise）；作業練習

expect   *v.* 預期；期望 *n.* expectation *adj.* expected

experience   *n.* 經驗 *v.* 歷經 *adj.* experienced 有經驗的

explain   *v.* 解釋 *n.* explanation

F

facility   *n.* 設施（一般用複數 facilities）

factory   *n.* 工廠

fail   *v.* 失敗 *n.* failure

fair   a. 公平的   n. 博覽會，展覽

fall   n. 跌倒；秋天（＝autumn）

falling   adj. 掉落的

family   n. 家庭；家人

famous   adj. 有名的（for）   n. fame 名聲

fan   n. 迷；扇子

farm   n. 農場（farmer 農夫）

fashion   n. 時裝（fashion show 時裝秀）

father   n. 父親

favorite   adj. 最喜愛的   n. 最喜愛的人、事、物

fax   n. v. 傳真

February   n. 二月

fill   v. 填滿（～with）

fine   v. 處以罰款   n. 罰金   adj. 好的；優質的

finish   v. 完成

fire   n. 火；火災   v. 解雇

firecrackers   n. 鞭炮

fireworks   n. 煙火

first   adj. adv. n. 第一（的）；首先（＝first of all）

fish   n. 魚；魚肉   v. 釣魚

fishburger   n. 魚堡

flight   n. 班機；飛行

floor   n. 地板

flower   n. 花

follow   v. 遵從，採用；追隨，跟蹤

following ＝ next   adj. 以下的；接下來的

forget   v. 忘記   adj. forgetful 健忘的

frankly   adv. 坦白地

Friday   n. 星期五

friend   n. 朋友

frighten   v. 驚嚇   adj. frightened 受到驚嚇的

frightening   adj. 令人害怕的

full-time ⟷ part-time   adj. adv. 全職的（地）⟷ 兼職的（地）

funny   adj. 好笑的   n. fun 樂趣

furniture   *n.* 傢俱（為集合名詞，須用單數動詞）

G

ghost   *n.* 鬼
girlfriend ⟷ boyfriend   *n.* 女友 ⟷ 男友
grade   *n.* 年級；等級；分數
graduate   *v.* 畢業（～from）   *n.* 畢業生
grandparents   *n.* 祖父母
grass   *n.* 青草，草地
gum = chewing gum   *n.* 口香糖

H

hardly   *adv.* 幾乎不
healthy   *adj.* 健康的   *n.* health 健康（in good health 健康的）
heavy   *adj.* 重的，胖的
help   *v. n.* 幫助   *adj.* helpful 有幫助的
hike   *v. n.* 健行（= hiking *n.*）（go on a hike = go hiking 去健行）
hire ⟷ fire   *v.* 雇用 ⟷ 解雇
hobby = interest   *n.* 嗜好
hold   *v.* 抓；抱；拿；舉行
holy = sacred   *adj.* 神聖的
homeless   *adj.* 無家可歸的
homework = assignment   *n.* 作業
honey   *n.* 蜂蜜；甜心
hope   *v. n.* 希望   *adj.* hopeful ⟷ hopeless 有希望的 ⟷ 沒有希望的
hospital   *n.* 醫院
hotel   *n.* 旅館，飯店
house   *n.* 房子
hug   *v. n.* 擁抱
humorous   *adj.* 幽默的   *n.* humor（a sense of humor 幽默感）

hungry   *adj.* 饑餓的；渴望的   *v. n.* hunger（～for）

hurry   *n. v.* 趕快（hurry up 趕快；in a hurry 匆忙）

hurt   *v.* 傷害；痛

husband ⟷ wife   *n.* 丈夫 ⟷ 妻子

however   *adv.* 然而

I

ideal   *adj.* 理想的

if = whether   *conj.* 假如；是否

illegal ⟷ legal   *adj.* 違法的 ⟷ 合法的

information   *n.* 訊息，資料，資訊（為集合名詞，須用單數動詞）

impolite ⟷ polite   *adj.* 沒禮貌的 ⟷ 客氣的，有禮貌的

important   *adj.* 重要的

include   *v.* 包括

independent ⟷ dependent   *adj.* 獨立的（～of） ⟷ 依賴的（～on）

India   *n.* 印度

in-flight   *adj.* 機上的，飛行中的

instead   *adv.* 作為替代；取代；而不是（～of）

interested   *adj.* 感到興趣的（～in）

interesting   *adj.* 有趣的（～to）

interest   *n.* 興趣；利益 *v.* 使…感到興趣

international   *adj.* 國際的

interview   *n. v.* 面試（= job interview）；（媒體）訪問

introduce   *v.* 介紹

J

January   *n.* 一月

item   *n.* 項目

join = take part in = participate in   *v.* 參加

journey   *n.* 旅程

July　　*n.* 七月

June　　*n.* 六月

K

kilometer = kilo　　*n.* 公里

knock　　*v. n.* 敲打（～on/at）

know　　*v.* 認識，知道

L

ladder　　*n.* 梯子

late　　*adj. adv.* 遲的（地）

law　　*n.* 法律

lazy　　*adj.* 懶惰的

leather　　*n.* 皮革

lend ⟷ borrow　　*v.* 借出（～to）⟷ 借入（～from）

let　　*v.* 讓（～V原形）

library　　*n.* 圖書館

likely　　*adj. adv.* 可能的（地）（～to）

London　　*n.* 倫敦

lonely = lonesome　　*adj.* 寂寞的

lost　　*adj.* 迷失的（= missing）；遺失的

loud　　*adj.* 大聲的

low-fat　　*adj.* 低脂的

M

make　　*v.* 製做；使（～V原形）

mall = shopping mall　　*n.* 大型購物中心

manager　　*n.* 經理

March   *n.* 三月

march   *v. n.* 行進

married ⟷ single   *adj.* 已婚的 ⟷ 單身的

marry   *v.* 娶；嫁   *n.* marriage 婚姻

math = mathematics   *n.* 數學

Massachusetts   *n.* 美國麻州

May   *n.* 五月；女子名

meal   *n.* 三餐之一

mean   *v.* 意味，意義   *adj.* 惡劣的

mention   *v.* 提及

message   *n.* 訊息，留言

    （take a message 代接留言，代為傳話；leave a message 留言）

member   *n.* 成員，會員

Mickey Mouse   *n.* 米老鼠

milkshake   *n.* 奶昔

mirror   *n.* 鏡子

miss   *v.* 思念；錯過

missing = lost   *adj.* 失蹤的，走失的

mistake   *n.* 錯誤（make a mistake 犯錯）

moment   *n.* 片刻

Monday   *n.* 星期一

mostly   *adv.* 多半，大部分

motorcycle = motorbike   *n.* 摩托車

mountain   *n.* 山（mountain climbing 爬山）

mouth   *n.* 嘴巴

move   *v.* 移動

movie = film   *n.* 電影

museum   *n.* 博物館

natural   *adj.* 自然的   *n.* nature

NBA = National Basketball Association   美國職業籃球協會

neighbor   *n.* 鄰居

nervous   *adj.* 緊張的

news   *n.* 新聞

newspaper   *n.* 報紙

next   *adj.* 下一個的

nice   *adj.* 美好的；親切的（～to）

noise   *n.* 噪音   *adj.* noisy   嘈雜的

nose   *n.* 鼻子

notice   *n.* 公告   *v.* 注意到

November   *n.* 十一月

O

October   *n.* 十月

offer   *v. n.* 提供；提議

office   *n.* 辦公室

once   *adv.* 曾經；一次；一旦

order   *v.* 點餐；訂貨   *n.* 秩序

outdoor   *adj.* 戶外的   *adv.* outdoors 在戶外

owner   *n.* 主人，擁有者；失主

P

paint   *n. v.* 油漆；上油漆；作畫

parents   *n.* 雙親

Paris   *n.* 巴黎

participate   參加（～in）

passage = paragraph   *n.* 段落（文章）

passenger   *n.* 乘客

patient   *adj.* 有耐心的   *n.* 病人   *n.* patience 耐心

pay   *v.* 付帳（～for）   *n.* 薪資

peace   *n.* 和平；平安

peanuts　　*n.* 花生（複數形）

performance　　*n.* 表演；表現

pet　　*n.* 寵物（pet shop = pet store 寵物店）

phone

　n. 電話　*v.* 打電話（= call (up) = telephon = ring = give... a ring）

photography　　*n.* 攝影（photo = photograph = picture 照片）

piece　　*n.* 片，碎片

place　　*n.* 地方　*v.* 放置

player　　*n.* 球員；玩家；播放器

pleasant　　*adj.* 令人愉快的，怡人的

please　　*v.* 取悅

pleasure　　*n.* 樂趣；榮幸

pocket　　*n.* 口袋

point　　*n.* 分數；要點　*v.* 指著（～at）；指出（～out）

policeman = police officer　　*n.* 警察（複數形為 policemen）

polite ⟷ impolite = rude

　adj. 客氣的，有禮貌的 ⟷ 不客氣的，沒禮貌的

pool = swimming pool　　*n.* 池子，游泳池

poor　　*adj.* 貧窮的；不好的

popular　　*adj.* 受歡迎的；普遍的（～with）

pork　　*n.* 豬肉

positive ⟷ negative　　*adj.* 正面的；肯定的 ⟷ 負面的；否定的

post　　*v.* 張貼；郵寄（= mail (美)）；郵政（= mail (美)）

postcard　　*n.* 名信片

postpone = put off　　*v.* 延期

potato　　*n.* 馬鈴薯

practice　　*v. n.* 練習

prefer　　*v.* 較喜歡

prepare　　*v.* 準備（～for）

present　　*n.* 禮物（= gift）　*adj.* 出席的，在場的　*v.* 出示；提出

pretty　　*adj.* 漂亮的　*adv.* 十分；非常

preview ⟷ review　　*v. n.* 預習 ⟷ 複習

price　　*n.* 價格

probably　　*adv.* 可能地（= likely *adv. adj.*）

progress   *n. v.* 進步；進行（in progress 進行中）

promise   *v. n.* 承諾，答應

proud   *adj.* 驕傲的（～of）

pub   *n.* 酒館（= public house）

public   *adj.* 公共的   *n.* 公共場所（in public 公開地；當眾）

punish   *v.* 處罰   *n.* punishment

purpose   *n.* 目的（on purpose 故意）

$\mathcal{R}$

rain   *n.* 雨   *v.* 下雨

raw   *adj.* 生的

reach   *v.* 與…連絡；搆到；到達（= get to = arrive in/at）

ready   *adj.* 準備好的（～for；～to + V）

realize   *v.* 了解；實現   *n.* realization

reason = cause   *n.* 原因

receive   *v.* 收到；接待

refrigeratior = fridge   *n.* 冰箱

relative   *n.* 親戚

religious   *adj.* 宗教的

remember   *v.* 記得；問候（～人 to...）

report   *n. v.* 報告；報案（～to）

research   *n. v.* 研究（researcher 研究員）

restaurant   *n.* 餐廳（cafe 小餐館）

restroom   *n.* 洗手間

return   *v. n.* 歸還；回來（～to... 回到…；～from... 從…回來）

review   *v. n.* 複習；評論

reward   *v. n.* 報酬

rice   *n.* 米；飯

ride   *v. n.* 騎乘

room   *n.* 房間

rule = regulation   *n.* 規則

run   *v.* 經營；跑步

S

sad   *adj.* 悲傷的

safety   *n.* 安全   *adj.* safe

salad   *n.* 沙拉

sale   *n.* 特賣（on sale），出售（for sale）

Saturday   *n.* 星期六

scared   *adj.* 感到害怕的（scary 可怕的）   *v.* scare 驚嚇

scary   *adj.* 令人害怕的，恐怖的

Scrabble   *n.* 填字遊戲，拼字遊戲

schoolwork   *n.* 學業

secret   *n.* 祕密（in secret 暗中）

seem   *v.* 似乎

semester = term   *n.* 學期

send   *v.* 寄；送

September   *n.* 九月

serve   *v.* 服務   *n.* service

several = some = a few   *adj.* 一些

share   *v.* 分享；共用

shirt   *n.* 襯衫

shorts   *n.* 短褲

show   *n.* 表演，節目   *v.* 表示；展現

sick   *adj.* 生病的；噁心的   *n.* sickness

silence   *n.* 安靜   *adj.* silent

since   *conj.* 自從；既然，因為   *prep.* 自從

sincerely   *adv.* 誠摯地，書末敬語

Singapore   *n.* 新加坡

single ⟷ married   *adj.* 單一的；單身的 ⟷ 已婚的（~to）

sign   *n.* 告示牌，招牌   *v.* 簽名

skirt   *n.* 裙子

sleep   *v. n.* 睡覺   *adj.* sleepy 想睡覺的（asleep 睡著的）

smart = clever   *adj.* 聰明的

smell   *v.* 聞；聞起來   *n.* 味道

smoke   *v.* 抽煙   *n.* 煙霧

smooth   *adj.* 順利的；平滑的

snacks   *n.* 點心，零食（複數形）

soccer   *n.* 足球

social   *adj.* 社會的，社交的   *n.* society

soda = soft drinks   *n.* 汽水

solve   *v.* 解決   *n.* solution

special   *adj.* 特別的   *n.* 特價品，特餐

spend   *v.* 花費（～... V-ing/on）

sport   *n.* 運動   *adj.* sports

spring   *n.* 春天

Sprite   *n.* 雪碧（飲料名）

stamp   *n.* 郵票

start   *v. n.* 開始（＝ begin *v.*；beginning *n.*）

statement   *n.* 敘述，聲明

stay   *v.* 停留；保持（＝ keep） *n.* 停留

steak   *n.* 牛排

still   *adv.* 仍然   *adj. adv.* 靜止的（地）

stinky   *adj.* 臭的

store = shop   *n.* 商店

strange   *adj.* 奇怪的；陌生的

student   *n.* 學生

studies   *n.* 研究   *v.* study

succeed   *v.* 成功（in） *n.* success   *adj.* successful

success   *n.* 成功；成功人士

suddenly = all of a sudden   *adv.* 突然

summer   *n.* 夏天

Sunday   *n.* 星期日

supermarket   *n.* 超市

surprise   *n.* 驚訝   *v.* 使…感到驚訝

surprising   *adj.* 令人驚訝的（～to）

surprised   *adj.* 感到驚訝的（～at）

sweater   *n.* 毛衣

sweet   *adj.* 甜美的；甜的；窩心的

sweetie = honey = darling　　*n.* 甜心

Sydney　　*n.* 雪梨（澳洲城市）

system　　*n.* 系統；制度

𝒯

Taimall　　台茂（位於桃園的一家大型購物中心）

talk　　*v. n.* 談話，聊天

talkative　　*adj.* 愛說話的，饒舌的

taste　　*v.* 嚐起來　*n.* 味道；品味

taxi = taxicab = cab　　*n.* 計程車

tea　　*n.* 茶（black tea 紅茶）

teacher　　*n.* 老師

terrible　　*adj.* 可怕的；糟糕的

test　　*n.* 考試　*v.* 試驗

theater　　*n.* 劇院（movie theater 電影院）

then　　*adv.* 然後；那時

therefore　　*adv.* 因此

thief　　*n.* 小偷（複數為 thieves）

thing　　*n.* 事物，東西

Thursday　　*n.* 星期四

title　　*n.* 標題；頭銜；書名；片名

tip　　*n.* 訣竅；建議；小費

today　　*n. adv.* 今日

tofu = bean curd　　*n.* 豆腐

together　　*adv.* 一起（～with 加上，與…一起）

Tokyo　　*n.* 東京

tomorrow　　*n. adv.* 明天

tonight　　*n. adv.* 今晚

top　　*n.* 頂端　*adj.* 頂級的

Toronto　　*n.* 多倫多

trouble　　*n.* 麻煩　*v.* 煩擾

truck　　*n.* 卡車

true　　*adj.* 真實的　*n.* truth 真實；真理
try　　*v. n.* 嘗試（= give... a try）；試圖（～to）
T-shirt　*n.* T恤
Tuesday　　*n.* 星期二

U

unexpected ⟷ expected　　*adj.* 出乎意料之外的 ⟷ 意料之中的
unforgettable　　*adj.* 難忘的
unhappy　　*adj.* 不快樂的；不滿意的
university　　*n.* 大學
unless　　*conj.* 除非…要不然
until = till　　*prep. conj.* 直到
usually = as usual = as a rule　　*adv.* 通常

V

vacation　　*n.* 假期　*v.* 渡假
video　　*n.* 錄影帶
visit　　*v. n.* 參觀；拜訪
voice　　*n.* 聲音

W

wallet　　*n.* 皮夾
wear　　*v.* 穿著　*n.* 服飾
weather　　*n.* 天氣
Wednesday　　*n.* 星期三
week　　*n.* 星期
weekend　　*n.* 週末
well-known = famous　　*adj.* 著名的

westerner   *n.* 西方人

wet   *adj.* 潮溼的

whether   *conj.* 是否

while   *conj.* 然而；當   *n.* 時間

whistle   *v. n.* （吹）口哨；（發）汽笛聲

wife ←→ husband   *n.* 妻子 ←→ 丈夫

wine   *n.* 葡萄酒

winter   *n.* 冬天

wonder   *v.* 納悶，想知道   *n.* 奇蹟

wonderful   *adj.* 奇妙的；極佳的

wonderland   *n.* 仙境

wood   *n.* 木頭（woods 樹林）

worth   *adj.* 值得…（～N/V-ing）

worried   *adj.* 擔心的（about）

write   *v.* 寫   *n.* writing   *n.* writer 作家（= author）

Y

yesterday   *n. adv.* 昨天

yellow   *n. adj.* 黃色的

Z

zero   *n.* 零

zoo   *n.* 動物園

A

a lot of = lots of = many = much = numerous　　很多

a sense of humor　　幽默感

above all = especially = most of all　　尤其，特別

according to　　根據

across from　　在…的對面

action movie　　動作片

after a while　　一會兒之後

after meals　　飯後

after school　　放學（後）

after work　　下班（後）

against the law　　違法

aged 5　　五歲

air conditioner　　冷氣機

alarm clock　　鬧鐘

all of a sudden = suddenly　　突然地

all the time = at all times = always　　總是

and so on = etc.　　等等

another time = some other time　　改天

around the corner　　在轉角；時間將至

arrive in/at = get to = reach　　到達

as for　　至於

as soon as = the moment　　一…就

as soon as posible = A.S.A.P.　　儘快

as usual = usually　　通常

ask for　　要求

ask sb. out　　約某人外出

at first　　起先

at first sight　　第一眼，初次見面（love at first sight 一見鍾情）

at last = finally　　終於

at once = right away = immediately　　立刻

at the beginning = at first　　起初，剛開始

at the moment = right now　　目前

at the same time = at one time = meanwhile = in the meantime　　同時

at times = sometimes = once in a while　　有時候

B

baseball fan　　（棒）球迷

baseball game　　棒球賽

basketball team　　籃球隊

be able to + V = can = be capable of + V-ing　　能夠

be about to (+ V)　　就要

be afraid of　　害怕

be allowed to　　可以，被允許去…

be aware of　　知道

be famous for = be well-known for　　以…聞名

be fond of　　喜歡

be full of = be filled with　　充滿

be interested in　　對…感到興趣

be located in　　座落於

be located near　　位於…附近

be out of　　用完

be proud of　　以…為榮

be used to + V-ing/N　　現在已習慣於

beauty contest　　選美

because of (+ N)　　由於

best friend　　至交，好友，死黨

best wishes　　獻上最佳祝福

black tea　　紅茶

both A and B　　A 和 B 兩者

bottled water　　瓶裝水

break down　　故障；崩潰

burn down　　燒毀

bus stop　　公車站（牌）

business hours　　營業時間
by mail　　藉由通信
by phone　　藉由電話
by the way　　順便一提；喔，對了
by way of = through　　藉由

C

call off = cancel　　取消
call on　　拜訪
call... for help　　打電話給…求救
care about　　在乎
care for = take care of　　照顧
CD player　　CD 播放器
China Airlines = CAL　　華航
clear up　　轉晴；清理；解除
collecting stamps　　集郵
come up with　　想出（計劃）
compare... with...　　比較…
compare... to　　比喻…為
corn soup　　玉米濃湯
credit card　　信用卡

D

day-care center = daycare center　　托兒所
deal with = handle　　處理
department store　　百貨公司
depend on　　依賴；視…而定
doze off　　打瞌睡
dress up (as)　　打扮（成）
drive... crazy　　使之瘋狂，把…逼瘋

drop a line + to + sb. = drop sb. a line　　捎個信給某人

E

each other = one another　　彼此
either A or B　　不是 A 就是B
even though = even if　　即使
except for　　除了…之外

F

factory worker　　作業員，（工廠）工人
fall asleep　　睡著
fall behind　　落後；不及；拖欠
fall in love (with)　　墜入愛河，愛上
fall out of　　從…掉出
falling star = shooting star　　流星
feel the same (way)　　有同感
figure out　　算出；了解
fill out = fill in = complete　　填寫
first of all = to begin with　　首先
flight attendant　　空服員；steward（空少），stewardess（空姐）
for (quite) a while　　（好長）一段時間
for a long time = for ages　　很久
for all = in spite of = despite　　儘管
for example = for instance　　例如
for fun　　為了好玩
for sure　　確定
for the time being　　暫時；目前
frankly speaking = to tell the truth　　老實說
French fries = fries　　薯條
from door to door　　挨家挨戶地

G

get along (with)　　與人相處得來；進展
get better　　好一點；變更好
get fatter and fatter　　變得愈來愈胖
get lost　　迷路（= lose one's way）；走開
get married　　結婚
get more and more popular　　變得愈來愈流行（普遍）
get off　　下車（公車、火車等）
get on　　上車（公車、火車等）
get rid of　　擺脫掉；戒掉
get to = arrive in/at = reach　　到達
get worse　　變更糟；更惡化
ghost story　　鬼故事，恐怖片
give up = quit　　放棄
go back to = return to　　回到
go hiking　　去健行
go swimming　　去游泳
go to the movies = go to a movie = see a movie　　看電影
go/be on a diet　　在節食

H

had to　　必須（用於過去時間，原形為 have to = must）
have a good time = have fun　　玩得愉快
have a sale　　舉行特賣會
hear from　　有…的訊息
here and there　　到處
hold on
　　等候（= just a minute/moment/second = one moment）；抓緊（to + N）
Hong Kong　　香港
hurry back to　　匆匆回到

hurry up   趕快

I

in a hurry = in haste   匆忙的（地）

in a mess   亂七八糟的

in a minute = in a second = in a while   一會兒

in advance = beforehand   預先，事先

in charge of = be responsible for   負責

in danger (of...)   陷入危險（有…的危險）

in fact = as a matter of fact = actually   事實上

in great shape   身體狀況良好的，很健康的

in luck ←→ out of luck   幸運的 ←→ 倒楣的

in one's free time   在某人有空時

in one's sixties   在某人六十幾歲時

in public   在公共場所

in spite of = despite   儘管

in the country = in the countryside ←→ in the city

    在鄉下 ←→ 在城市

in the long run = at last = finally   終究；最終

in the mountains   在山上

in the way   妨礙

in town   鎮上，本地

in vain   無效，枉然

insist on   堅持；強調

instead of   代替；而不是…

invite... over   邀…過來

J

just a moment = just a second = just a minute = one moment   等一下

$\mathcal{K}$

keep an eye on　　看顧；注意

keep in mind = bear in mind = remember　　記住

keep in touchwith someone　　與…保持聯繫

keep off = keep out of　　遠離

keep on = go on = continue　　繼續；一直

laugh at = make fun of　　嘲笑

$\mathcal{L}$

learn... by heart　　記住

leave a message　　留言

leave for　　前往

leave someone alone　　不打擾

less than　　少於

let off　　發射，放（鞭炮）；讓…下車

likes and dislikes　　好惡

listen to　　聽（音樂等）

long time no see　　好久不見

look after = take care of = watch over　　照顧；照料

look at　　看著（某人、某物）

look for = search for = hunt for　　尋找

look forward to (+ V-ing/N)　　期待；盼望

look into　　調查

look up　　查看

look up to = respect　　尊敬

Los Angeles　　洛杉磯

lose weight ⟷ put on weight　　減重，減肥 ⟷ 增胖

lots of = a lot of　　很多

love letter　　情書

love story　　愛情故事，文藝片

lucky money   *n.* 壓歲錢

M

mail carrier = postman = mailman   郵差
make a date   計畫約會
make a mistake   犯錯
make faces   做鬼臉
make friends (with)   和⋯交朋友
make fun of = laugh at   取笑
make it = do it = succeed   成功，做到
make out   辨認；理解
make sure   確定；確認
make up   編造；補足
make up one's mind (to + V)   下決定；下決心
most of all = above all   尤其
movie star   電影明星
movie theater   電影院

N

named Kenny   名叫肯尼
National Palace Museum   國立故宮博物院
neither A nor B   非A亦非B
New York   紐約
next to = beside   在⋯的旁邊／隔壁
no doubt   難怪
not only... but also...   不但⋯而且⋯
not... any more = not... any longer = no more = no longer   不再
not... at all   一點也不

O

of course = sure = certainly　　當然
on his way to school　　他上學途中
on my way home　　在我回家的路上
on one's own　　獨立的（地）
on one's/the way　　在路上（to）；馬上
on purpose　　故意
on weekend　　在週末
once a week　　每週一次
once in a while　　有時候；偶而
one moment = just a second = just a minute = just a moment　　等一下
onion ring(s)　　洋蔥圈
ought to = should　　應該
out of date = out of fashion　　過時的
out of one's mind　　瘋了
out of order　　故障
out of the question　　不可能的；辦不到的；不必談的
outdoor concert　　露天／戶外音樂會（演唱會）
outside of class　　課外

P

pet shop = pet store　　寵物店
pick out = choose = select　　選擇，挑出
pick up　　接送；拾起；取件
pizza store = pizzeria　　披薩店
play computer games　　玩電腦遊戲
play tricks on　　詐騙；開玩笑
play video games　　打電動
point at　　指著
point out　　指出

police officer = policeman　　警察
pop music = popular music　　流行音樂
post office　　郵局
prefer A to B　　喜歡A甚於B
prevent... from　　阻止；妨礙
put away　　收拾
put down = write down　　寫下
put off　　延期
put on　　穿戴上
put out　　撲滅，熄滅
put up with = stand = bear　　容忍；忍受

R

red envelope　　紅包
result from　　因而引起；因而發生
result in　　導致…結果
right away = at once = immediately　　立刻
run into = bump into = run across = meet... by chance　　不期而遇，撞見
run out of　　用完
run over　　輾過
run through　　衝過，闖（紅燈）

S

San Francisco　　三藩市，舊金山
say hello to = say hi to = greet　　向…問候
school bus　　校車
show off　　炫耀；賣弄
sleep late　　晚起
so far　　迄今，到目前為止
stay up = sit up　　熬夜

stinky tofu　　臭豆腐

stop... from = prevent... from　　禁止，阻撓

study for　　準備（考試…）

such as = like　　例如，像是

surf the Internet = surf/use the net　　上網

swimming pool　　游泳池

T

take a message　　代接留言，代為傳話

take a nap　　小睡片刻

take a trip (to + 地點)　　旅行

take a vacation　　渡假

take action　　採取行動

take care of = look after = watch over　　照顧

take notes　　做筆記

take off　　脫下；起飛

take one's time　　不急，慢慢來

take out　　拿出，掏出

take part in = participate in　　參加

take photos = take pictures　　照相

take place = be held　　發生；舉行

take the medicine　　吃藥

take turns　　輪流

talk/be on the phone　　講電話

That's it.　　就這樣。沒錯。

the day after tomorrow　　後天

the day before yesterday　　前天

the Internet= the following day　　網際網路

the next day　　隔天

the other day = a few days ago　　前幾天

the police　　警方（須用複數動詞）

(in) the same way　　同樣地

think... over = consider　考慮

thousands of　數以千計的

three times　三次

to one's surprise　令…感到驚訝的是

to tell the truth = to be honest (with you) = to be frank (with you)
　老實說

tow away　拖吊

train station　火車站

try on　試穿

turn down　（將聲音或光線等）調小或調弱；拒絕（= reject）

turn off　關掉（燈或電器用品等）

turn on　打開（燈或電器用品等）

turn out (to be)　結果變成

turn over = overturn　翻轉

turn up　（將聲音或光線等）調大或調強

U

up to date　最新的；時新的

ups and downs　起伏；盛衰；沉浮；滄桑

used to (+ V原形)　過去的習慣或事實

V

Valentine's Day　情人節

vendening machine　自動販賣機

W

wake up　醒來；叫醒

wash the dishes = do the dishes　洗碗

watch out (for) = look out (for) = be careful (of)　　小心

What happened?　　怎麼了？發什什麼事？

What's more　　再者

what's worse　　更糟的是

whether or not = whether... or not = whether　　是否

wish me luck　　祝我好運

work on　　研究；練習；解決

不規則動詞變化表

原形/現在式	過去式	過去分詞	中文字義
be (am/is/are)	was/were	been	是；成為；（存）在
become	became	become	變成；變得
begin	began	begun	開始
beat	beat	beaten	打；擊；打敗
bite	bit	bitten	咬
blow	blew	blown	吹
break	broke	broken	打破；打斷
bring	brought	brought	帶來
build	built	built	建造
burn	burnt/burned	burnt/burned	燒；燒掉；燒焦
buy	bought	bought	購買
catch	caught	caught	抓（到）；搭（車）；接（住）
choose	chose	chosen	選擇
come	came	come	來（到）
cost	cost	cost	花費
cut	cut	cut	切，砍；割傷
dig	dug	dug	挖（出）
do	did	done	做
draw	drew	drawn	畫；拉；提領
dream	dreamt/dreamed	dreamt/dreamed	作夢；夢見
drink	drank	drunk	喝
drive	drove	driven	開車；駕駛
eat	ate	eaten	吃
fall	fell	fallen	落下；跌倒
feed	fed	fed	餵
feel	felt	felt	感覺；覺得；摸起來（後接形容詞）
fight	fought	fought	打架；吵架
find	found	found	尋找；找到
fly	flew	flown	飛
forget	forgot	forgot/forgotten	忘記
forgive	forgave	forgiven	原諒

原形/現在式	過去式	過去分詞	中文字義
get	got	got/gotten	得到；取得；變得
give	gave	given	給
go	went	gone	去；開始；變得
grow	grew	grown	成長；變得
have	had	had	有；吃；喝；使
hear	heard	heard	聽（到）
hide	hid	hidden	躲；藏
hit	hit	hit	打；擊中
hold	held	held	握；抓；拿；保持
hurt	hurt	hurt	傷害；受傷
keep	kept	kept	保持
know	knew	known	知道；了解；認識
lead	led	led	領導；引導；過著
learn	learnt/learned	learnt/learned	學習；知道；得知
leave	left	left	離開；留給；使得
lend	lent	lent	借出；借給（～to）
let	let	let	讓
lose	lost	lost	遺失；迷失；輸掉
make	made	made	做；製做；使
mean	meant	meant	意為；有意
meet	met	met	遇見；會面
mistake	mistook	mistaken	誤解；誤認為
oversleep	overslept	overslept	睡過頭
pay	paid	paid	付；付出
prove	proved	proven	證明
put	put	put	放；置於
quit	quit/quitted	quit/quitted	戒掉；辭職；退出；放棄
read	read	read	讀；唸
ride	rode	ridden	騎；乘
ring	rang	rung	鈴響；按鈴；打電話
rise	rose	risen	上升；起立
run	ran	run	跑；經營

原形/現在式	過去式	過去分詞	中文字義
say	said	said	說
see	saw	seen	看；看見；了解
sell	sold	sold	賣；銷售
send	sent	sent	發送；郵寄；派遣
set	set	set	放；置；設定
shake	shook	shaken	搖動；握（手）
shine	shone/shined	shone/shined	照耀／擦亮
show	showed	shown/showed	顯示；出示；放映
shut	shut	shut	關上；合上
sing	sang	sung	唱歌
sink	sank/sunk	sunk/sunken	沉；使下沉
sit	sat	sat	坐下
sleep	slept	slept	睡覺
smell	smelt/smelled	smelt/smelled	聞；聞起來（後接形容詞）
speak	spoke	spoken	說，講
spend	spent	spent	花費；花時間
stand	stood	stood	站立；忍受
steal	stole	stolen	偷竊
strike	struck	struck/striken	打，擊
sweep	swept	swept	打掃；掃除
swim	swam	swum	游泳
take	took	taken	拿；帶；乘坐；花時間
teach	taught	taught	教書；教導
tear	tore	torn	撕；撕開
tell	told	told	告訴；辨別（～from）
think	thought	thought	想；考慮；認為
throw	threw	thrown	丟，投，擲
understand	understood	understood	了解
wake	woke/waked	waken/waked	醒來
wear	wore	worn	穿；戴
win	won	won	贏；賺取
write	wrote	written	寫

Notes

_____

_____

_____

_____

_____

_____

_____

_____

_____

_____

_____

_____

Notes

_____

_____

_____

_____

_____

_____

_____

_____

_____

_____

_____

_____

Notes

_____

_____

_____

_____

_____

_____

_____

_____

_____

_____

_____

Notes

_____

_____

_____

_____

_____

_____

_____

_____

_____

_____

_____

_____

國家圖書館出版品預行編目資料

全民英檢初級保證班／閱讀與寫作（題
庫）／初碧華著.--二版--.--臺北市：
書泉出版社,2023.09
面； 公分
ISBN 978-986-451-340-6（平裝）
1.英語 2.問題集

805.1892　　　　　　　112014836

3AS5

全民英檢初級保證班：
閱讀與寫作（題庫）

作　　者 ― 初碧華(452)

發 行 人 ― 楊榮川

總 經 理 ― 楊士清

總 編 輯 ― 楊秀麗

副總編輯 ― 黃惠娟

責任編輯 ― 陳巧慈

插　　畫 ― 依果

美術編輯 ― 米栗設計工作室

出 版 者 ― 書泉出版社

地　　址：106台北市大安區和平東路二段339號4樓

電　　話：(02)2705-5066　　傳　　真：(02)2706-6100

網　　址：https://www.wunan.com.tw

電子郵件：shuchuan@shuchuan.com.tw

劃撥帳號：01303853

戶　　名：書泉出版社

法律顧問　林勝安律師

出版日期　2006年 3 月初版一刷
　　　　　2015年10月初版八刷
　　　　　2023年 9 月二版一刷

定　　價　新臺幣320元

經典永恆·名著常在

五十週年的獻禮——經典名著文庫

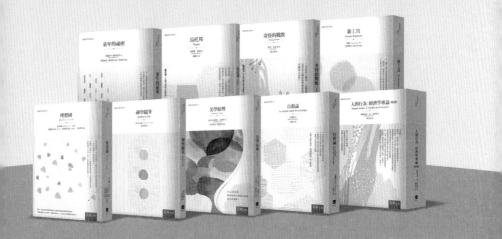

五南，五十年了，半個世紀，人生旅程的一大半，走過來了。

思索著，邁向百年的未來歷程，能為知識界、文化學術界作些什麼？

在速食文化的生態下，有什麼值得讓人雋永品味的？

歷代經典·當今名著，經過時間的洗禮，千錘百鍊，流傳至今，光芒耀人；

不僅使我們能領悟前人的智慧，同時也增深加廣我們思考的深度與視野。

我們決心投入巨資，有計畫的系統梳選，成立「經典名著文庫」，

希望收入古今中外思想性的、充滿睿智與獨見的經典、名著。

這是一項理想性的、永續性的巨大出版工程。

不在意讀者的眾寡，只考慮它的學術價值，力求完整展現先哲思想的軌跡；

為知識界開啟一片智慧之窗，營造一座百花綻放的世界文明公園，

任君遨遊、取菁吸蜜、嘉惠學子！